WHO'S KILLING THE GREAT WRITERS OF AMERICA?

A SATIRE

SUE GRAFTON

STEPHEN KING

DANIELLE STEEL

CURTIS SITTENFELD

TOM CLANCY

BY ROBERT KAPLOW

PHOENIX BOOKS

Portions of this novel originally appeared in THE ATLANTIC under the title *Jarhead Meets Flattop: Dick Tracy in Fallujah.*

ISBN: 1-59777-547-9
Library of Congress Cataloging-In-Publication Data Available

Book Design by: Sonia Fiore

Printed in the United States of America

Phoenix Books
9465 Wilshire Boulevard, Suite 315
Beverly Hills, CA 90212

10 9 8 7 6 5 4 3 2 1

BY THE SAME AUTHOR

Werewolves of Linden

Hey, Primo! The Primo Levi Musical

I'm Dickens; He's Faulkner

Brave New Wiener (with Eric Schlosser)

Pez: It Will Come Back to You

When Your Balls Hit the Floor Like a B-54 and Other Verse for Children

Seltzer Boy: Social Criticism and the Lyrics of Allan Sherman

Hanna-Barbera's Literary Classics:

    Beckett's *Waiting for El Kabong*

    Mozart's *The Marriage of Babalooie*

    (conducted by Esa-Pekka Kabibble)

Who's Killing the Great Writers of America?

a satire concerning (among others) Sue Grafton,
Gustave Flaubert, René Magritte, Arthur Conan
Doyle, Cole Porter, Steve Martin, Claire Danes,
Bugs Bunny, Archie Rice, Chung Ling Soo, Benny
Hill, Jane Austen, Vladimir Nabokov, Basil
Rathbone, Stephen King, George W. Bush, Tabitha
King, Arthur Miller, J.D. Salinger, John Updike,
Cormac McCarthy, Brooklyn Decker, Danielle Steel,
Curtis Sittenfeld, Mitch Albom, Victor Hugo, F.
Scott Fitzgerald, Gérard Depardieu, Carson
McCullers, Wally Lamb, Matthew McConaughey, César
Ritz, Alice Munro, Daniel Menaker, Jennifer Egan,
Virginia Woolf, Janet Maslin, François Truffaut,
Ernst Lubitsch, Truman Capote, A.O. Scott, Spike
Lee, T. Coraghessan Boyle, Robert James Waller,
Munro Leaf, Michiko Kakutani, Georgia O'Keeffe,
Diane Sawyer, Emma Peel, Paul Simon, Tom Clancy,
Patrick McGoohan, Jerry Orbach, Alfred Hitchcock,
Charles Trenet, Eric Lustbader, Simon Oakland,
John le Carré, Hugo Chavez, Makdi-El Sadr, Amy
Goodman, Noam Chomsky, Frank Rich, Yo-Yo-Ma, the
Marquis de Sade, Charles Ludlam, Sir Walter Scott,
Thomas Heggen, Steven Spielberg, Bernard Herrmann,
Jack Webb, Hideo Nakata, Gore Verbinski, Shirley
Jackson, Laura Nyro, Bobby Darin, Johnny Mercer,
Robot Commando, William Gibson, Mildred Bailey,
Dr. Ronald Hoffman, and the Ink Spots.

to Michael Townsend

Who's Killing the Great Writers
of America? is a work of
fiction. Although the story is
set against a background of
actual people and places, those
people and places have been
completely reimagined in the
spirit of parody and burlesque.
—R.K.

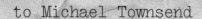

Hip the canary,
It'll be scary,
After the warm-up.
—Johnny Mercer

ONE

DIARRHEA ON THE ORIENT EXPRESS

As she studied an elderly woman with a walker, Sue Grafton thought: *We watch our friends, one by one, grow sick and die, and then, one day, they watch us grow sick and die.*

Grafton shook the thought out of her head. This was supposed to be her birthday trip. She turned for more life-affirming language to her paperback of *Madame Bovary:*

> *...no one can ever express the exact measure
> of his needs, his conceptions or his sorrows—
> and human speech is like a cracked pot on
> which we beat out rhythms for bears to dance
> to when what we really long for is to make
> music that will wring tears from the stars.*

Ain't that the Goddamn truth, she thought. She sat in the Statione Ferovia S. Lucia in Venice. In front of a marble rectangular column, rising out of a mountain of luggage, stood a brass frame. It bore the sign: *Venice Simplon Orient-Express—Boarding Time.* Beneath the words was a drawing of a clock: pale blue hands against a darker blue background. The clock indicated 10:25. Next to the sign stood a large bald man in a khaki short-sleeved shirt talking on a cell phone. His hand obscured his face, and the sun glinted off his aluminum attaché case.

He'll be the killer, thought Grafton whose mind was nearly always working in that direction. Kinsey will meet him on the train.... No, there was a more interesting-looking guy behind him: a muscular young black man in a white shirt with a perfectly sculpted face. He wore a silver bracelet.

Kinsey will meet *him* on the train. He's the rap star. Gives her a CD with a picture of him on the front dressed in a white suit, black tie, and a black cashmere scarf. He's holding a wireless microphone. The title of the CD is *Big Nig*.

"I don't know how to say this," Kinsey will say, raising her eyebrow. "But isn't that a little, how do I say it, in terrible taste?"

"Terrible taste?" asks the man.

"Big Nig, isn't that a little self-deprecating? It's like...I don't know, but you'd never hear a Jewish lesbian pop star calling herself Kike Dyke."

"No, no, no, Kinsey." His voice is softened by an English working-class accent. "You've got it all wrong. It's big *Naij*—my name is Nigel. Soft g. Long i. Big Ni-gel."

"Oh, my God, I am *so* sorry."

Grafton looks at the CD. The label is Engorged Phallus Records. The blurb reads: "A semenal work"—Kelefa Sanneh, *NY Times*.

All right, maybe that angle won't work.

Too offensive too early.

Grafton looked back up towards the marble column to see that the black man had disappeared into the crowd. *One second you're the star of my book,* she thought, *and the next second you don't even exist.* It certainly was a strange moment when you crossed paths with a writer who was "gathering." She'd borrow, at least, that silver bracelet....

She'd make it a white gold—18-karat—engraved identification bracelet. And they find it next to the dead body where it has conveniently fallen in the struggle. *Perhaps too conveniently,* thought Inspector Magritte, the celebrated surrealist detective. The overweight American mystery writer's body lay hideously contorted on the railroad tracks.

Using pale lavender latex gloves Magritte picked up the identification bracelet. On one side was engraved *Nigel*. On the other side was engraved: *From Everyone at E.P.*

"Engorged phallus?" asked the inspector's willowy blonde assistant.

"No," said Magritte. "I'm actually feeling quite relaxed." He continued to examine the large cement sewage drain next to the body. *"Ce n'est pas une pipe!"* he suddenly cried, as a locomotive roared out the fireplace, destroying his bowler....

Grafton shook her head.

She had to stop her mind.

Maybe she really *had* written herself out.

Her heart told her she should have stopped with *Z is for Zero-Coupon Bond*, but, no, her cheerily well-heeled publisher had pushed and hammered and harangued her. She groaned a little as she reread the typed letter which now served as a bookmark in her *Madame Bovary*.

...so glad to hear you have finally begun work on AA IS FOR AARDVARK. Everyone in office convinced this will be your biggest hit yet. Possible title for later book in series: DD IS FOR DOUBLE D. Psychotic Beverly Hills surgeon makes women's breasts so huge they suffocate as they sleep. Funny movie possibilities.

All best,

Jerry Goniff, president,

Posthumous Press

P.S. AARDVARK already in spring catalogue. Best pre-order since W IS FOR WANK.

She groaned again. *AA is for Aardvark.* How on earth could she get a book out of that?

When she'd visited New York last month, having lunch with her editor and publicist from Posthumous at some lovely Italian place on Ninth, she'd been quietly preoccupied with the problem of inventing a story that could even remotely accommodate the title *AA is for Aardvark*. And how would the third series start? *AAA is for Penlight Battery?* …No wonder Sir Arthur Conan Doyle had finally killed off Sherlock Holmes. She could still recite from memory the last sentence of "The Final Problem," still loved the music of that closing cadence: an elegy for "him whom I shall ever regard as the best and wisest man whom I have ever known." *A beautifully-shaped sentence*, Grafton thought. Right down to the double use of the word "whom." That stilted, formal word choice gave it the swallowed choke in the throat, the Victorian gentleman in his tweeds, muttonchops, and tight wool necktie holding back his tears as he closed the weighty tome on Mr. Sherlock Holmes—his limits. Of course the great clamorous Victorian public had pushed and hammered and harangued poor Conan Doyle until the doctor relented— propped up the corpse for thirteen more stories in *The Return of Sherlock Holmes*, two remaining novels, and two more story collections: *His Last Bow* and the *Case Book of Sherlock Holmes*. Poor Conan Doyle! It was like *Weekend at Bernie's, Part 35*. And poor Holmes! His corpse dressed up in an Hawaiian shirt and dark glasses, somebody shaking his arm goodbye.

She hoped to God Kinsey wouldn't exit that way. Have the decency to send her hurling over Reichenbach Falls locked in the arms of her Professor Moriarty! Consign them both to a watery eternity. Maybe Kinsey's final story could be called *Her Last Bow*, but the "bow" wouldn't be a stage bow; it would be a pink ribbon tied in a bow. A suitably feminine touch for the finale of "perhaps the most likable female private eye in the business." (*The Boston Globe*) Actually, Grafton thought, there was something slightly dismissive and repellent about the word "likable." Was Emma Bovary likable? It was precisely her irresponsibility and selfishness that made her so compelling. The last thing on earth she could be called was "likable." *The Sisterhood of the Shared Sanitary Napkin* was likable. *Mystic Pizza* was likable. *The Babysitter's Club* and those endless chick books with the pink and green covers and the pictures of the shopping bags…*that* crap was likable. Kinsey deserved better.

Reader, I killed her.

Maybe this *would* be the trip where cruel Sue Grafton murdered her forever-thirty-something heroine.

A chime sounded in that sunlight-soaked train station, and a pleasant female voice announced in Italian, English, French, and German that the Orient Express Venice-to-Paris overnight was now boarding.

"Could we possibly ask you to take our picture?"

It was a young-looking couple: he in a dark linen shirt; she in a black sundress.

"I'd love to," said Grafton.

Some kind of anniversary, she thought.

The couple stood smiling in the doorway of Car E— the train all blue and brass. At their feet the brass step read *Metropolitan Carriage.*

And so 1/24th of a second of their lives was captured on a 35mm strip of old-fashioned film. They thanked her and moved off towards their berth with a certain ardent urgency, the young man steering the woman's shoulders ahead of him.

Fellatio on the Orient Express, Grafton thought.

It was hot on the train. Seriously hot. It was August 23rd. Her original plan had been to travel on April 23rd— Shakespeare's birthday and the day before her own. She was four months late, as usual, but she was still pleased by the basic design of the trip: to be 3,000 miles from Santa Barbara, California: to be alone on this exotic train, rumbling mightily through the Alps, west towards Paris. It was a journey that would take almost exactly 24 hours. Who knew what could happen in 24 hours? She'd get the idea for her next book? She'd have a torrid affair with Big Nigel and his Engorged Phallus, while the train whistle drowned out her ecstasy? (Train plunging into the tunnel.) She'd find *something*... maybe just the color, the texture...or maybe she'd actually find the eccentric American who'd be perfect for the novel or the British ex-colonel: slightly drunk, cruel, heartless— traveling with his poor, timid, green-eyed daughter who'd been disappointing him for 32 years.

The temperature on the train was in the mid 80s, and it felt oppressively humid. "No," explained Paolo, the olive-skinned attendant, "there ees no air conditioning." Paolo, in his blue and gold *Grans Express Europeans* uniform wore his long, ash-blonde hair pulled back in a ponytail. His left ear was spiked with a gold earring. Grafton thought: *College student*. Universite de Venizia. This is how he and his lecherous Neapolitan friends spent their summers, and they met at the end of the run to compare notes on how many euros they could steal and how many lonely female tourists they could pleasure.

Oh, well, poor toothy Paolo was probably too young for the elegant, aging, wealthy Ms. Grafton—a woman, after all, in her late sixties. Soon would come her crossover into...what? The Sagging Seventies? The Simple-Minded Seventies? The Saliva-Dripping Seventies? Next year instead of taking a trip on the Orient Express she'd be taking a trip down the hallway of the Orient Express Assisted Living

Center. (Suites for the Memory-Impaired Available.) And she'd have a fantastic culinary choice for lunch between the Venezia Three-Bean Salad (kidney, navy, fava), the Zurich Three-Bean Salad (kidney, navy, fava), and the Paris Three-Bean Salad (kidney and fava only—*mon dieu,* they had to save *some* money, *yes!*)

Paolo handed her a Yale lock key attached by a beaded chain to a silver disk stamped 3482 (the car number) and 1 (the room number.) "If der is anyting what I can do, you for simply ask. Anyting."

"*Mille grazie,* Paolo."

"*Prego.* I come back wit your luggage."

He sauntered down the corridor and, in one of those deliciously slow-motion moments, offered her an entirely flirtatious smile over his left shoulder.

"Youth," she said quietly, "might be the only truth." It was a line from a song lyric she'd written in her twenties. This was back when she was living in Kentucky; when she had actually considered becoming a professional lyricist. At the time *youth might be the only truth* had seemed as if it might have been a truism. Now it seemed so far from the truth it was laughable. She shook her head at the memory of her wayward past: married at 18 to Micky Magruder...what on earth had she been thinking? Then James L. Flood and two children and two years and sitting in that suffocating, linoleum-lined kitchen thinking: *What the fuck am I doing here?* Then the second marriage (Last Exit Before Disaster) to Al Schmidt and the drinking and the lying and her last pregnancy. She remembered their apartment with the portable clothes washer jammed next to the kitchen sink; the hose would suddenly pop and dump thirteen gallons of warm soapy water on the floor until Nina downstairs called hysterically that it was pouring through her ceiling.

Grafton had told Al she was pregnant in that kitchen. His reaction: "Great. One more thing we can't afford."

It was genuinely amazing to think of the chain of events that had silently conspired to bring her to this solitary train trip. Amazing and a little sad.

The corridors of the Orient Express were carpeted in dark blue; the old-fashioned sliding windows to the right; the rooms to the left. The walls were polished wood the color of sweet potatoes, edged in green parquetry. The same parquetry appeared on the doors in a thin green diamond. The corridor was narrow, and the ceiling low, white, and illuminated with a series of small tulip-shaped lamps.

Grafton thought to herself that people must have been so *small* in the 1920s: these British rosebuds off on their Grand Tours with their massive, unwieldy steamship trunks and their massive, unwieldy mothers. This claustrophobic corridor and this unendurable heat had constituted luxury traveling! It really had been another world.

Paolo dragged her suitcase down the hall sideways. He unlocked the door to #1. "Do you know who iz on the train today? Steve Martin."

"The comedian?"

"Yes, I carried his banjo."

"His banjo? He's going to perform?"

"He might. After dinner. In ze bar. Iz frequent travel on zeez train. You probably meet him at dinner. He want to meet you."

"Me?"

"You are famous writer, signora Grafton. Your books very popular in Italy."

"Really?"

"H is for Homo-chee-day!"

Grafton laughed. "It sounds so much better the way you say it."

She had prepared to give him a two-euro coin. She doubled it.

"H is for Homo-chee-day," he repeated with delight as he left. There was something in his slightly criminal smile that reminded her of a pirate. Maybe it was just that gold earring. Irrational desire swept over her.

"Pirate Paolo," said Grafton to herself. "Hey, Paolo, if you swab my deck, I'll let you bury your treasure."

She laughed at this private raunchy voice she rarely acknowledged. Maybe she'd invent a character for that voice. A sidekick for Kinsey. An earthy rock 'n' roll bar waitress with torn fishnet stockings.

And maybe what she felt for Paolo wasn't irrational desire at all. Maybe it was purely rational lust. Maybe it was the return of that bad girl she'd been when she was sixteen. That version of Grafton who had preened and pouted and relentlessly studied herself in the mirror; had walked barefoot down the streets until strange men honked their horns. *That* girl had been politely put away in a drawer: pressed, trimmed, laundered, declawed—then hung in the mothball-smelling cabinet called Responsibility. Her marriage to Steve, her children, her book signings, her loyal public. Locked away for forty years until the bad girl was angry, frustrated, and ready to explode; sick of being silenced.

Maybe that was the real point of this trip. To feel *that* girl again.

She was so hot she felt she must be sick. The train couldn't have been that warm. The Italian cities rolled noisily past—hot grit and glitter and the smell of the train engine: Padova, Vicenza, Verona, Trento, Bolzano.... They were nearing Austria but it still didn't feel any cooler. Her compartment was a little jewel box—a boiling-hot jewel box. The window could be opened for air, but the thunder of the wheels was instantly headache-inducing. The room's one concession to technology was a small electric fan with blue plastic blades over the door—next to the emergency handle. The walls were dark wood and edged in the same green parquetry as the hallway: wooden diamonds that resembled a row of teeth. The bed could be lowered from the wall like an ironing board on a cloth strap. Outlined in green wood was a hexagonal mirror, and opening like a sort of Art Deco phone booth was a tiny sink, a small round shaving mirror, and some drinking glasses mounted on silver wall brackets. There was no toilet. That was down the hall.

The most charming nook in this little jewel box was the seat by the window. It was amply upholstered: white and pink flowers against a black background, and it abutted a tiny writing desk in front of the window. On the writing desk stood a single silver reading lamp with a rose-colored silk shade. Grafton imagined Cole Porter sitting with his legal pad at the tiny desk listing rhymes for "can-can," as the bright Italian cities flickered by outside.

Hindustan can

African can

A wave of nausea suddenly passed over Grafton, and her face was moist with sweat.

Must have been the mussels....

She'd eaten by herself the previous night in Venice, and she'd been seated, as usual, in the worst seat in the Ristorante Antico Martini, bravely pretending to be doing the crossword in the *International Tribune*, bravely pretending to be at ease with herself. She sat with her thick legs and manifestly graying hair.... And, yes, she'd *insisted* on taking this trip alone. It wasn't midlife crisis; it was three-quarters-life crisis. Her 68th birthday. Stephen Hughes, her husband of 24 years, had arranged the whole thing, had paid for it, had *pushed* her to follow her little birthday dream. The poor bastard. He probably wanted to be alone as much as she did—or as much as she *thought* she did. Alone seemed so alluring in the abstract.

"No cell phones," Stephen had dictated. "Unless it's an absolute emergency. Really. Be totally on your own for a few days. In a country where you barely speak the language...." He had laughed.

She found herself sitting alone at eight o'clock at a largely empty restaurant in Venice. At the party table in the center of the dining room sat the theatre director Harold Prince, his eyeglasses famously tilted on top of his head. Next to him sat Joel Grey, the actor, and four wives or friends. Prince was loud, laughing and flamboyant, a man used to being the center of the room. He noticed her sitting by the back mural, and she thought he might actually call her over: "My dear, you look so lonely sitting over there; would you care to join us?"

She'd move to the table. "I'm an American writer."

"What a coincidence. I'm an American reader."

And by the time the dinner was over Prince would have decided to make a musical about her famous female detective (*K is for Kinsey*); he'd put in a call to Sondheim—if he couldn't get Sondheim he'd get Meatloaf. He was thinking Patty Lupone as Kinsey—if he couldn't get Lupone he'd get Harvey Fierstein.

But poor Grafton had sat alone, and stayed alone, eating three terrible, poisonous-tasting mussels in a green sauce that looked like anti-freeze. She watched the *vitality* of Prince's table with envy. Vitality felt like an increasingly precious commodity in her life.

That evening, after dinner in Venice, she'd stayed up late in her hotel room. The hotel was located directly on the canal, but, of course, her room faced the wrong side and her entire view of romantic Venice consisted of a geometric intersection of roofs, tiled with what looked like red clay pipes cut in half. The TV in her room was showing *Shopgirl* with Steve Martin and Claire Danes, and while she couldn't understand the Italian overdubbed dialogue what she *could* understand, immediately, was the artistic lunacy of pairing Martin (60?) with Danes (26?). In close-up, Danes's hair burned reddish brown; her eyes lit with rage, hurt, joy. And there was Martin looking sickly and desiccated, his eyes like tiny raisins. There was something creepy and slightly pornographic in the relationship, as if Martin's character had used expensive wine and Armani dresses to buy himself a young woman.

A loud knocking at her compartment door.

Then the handle turned; she'd left it unlocked, and there in the corridor stood Steve Martin.

The actual Steve Martin. Age 62. He wore a comedian's prop arrow-sticking-through-the-head.

"Excuse me, madam, my name is the Lone Ranger. Have you seen any Indians going by this way?" His eyes seemed to catch sight of someone down the hall. "Excuse me; I'll be right back." He shut the door, but she could still hear his voice, cadenced like Jack Benny. "Oh, *Tonto!*"

Now six more loud knocks—knocked to the rhythm of shave-and-a-haircut-two—and where the word "bits" should have occurred there was a loud metallic snap followed by a *(yow!)* howling of pain.

The door pushed open again, and there stood Martin with a huge mousetrap closed on his right hand, elaborately waving it in pain.

"Why do they *insist* on using these?" Then, in a kind of comic freeze-frame, he stopped all movement, stared at her with a goony expression, and let out a loud Woody-Woodpecker laugh. Actually it sounded like the early Bugs Bunny, the large, loping rabbit of "Elmer's Candid Camera." Martin looked right at her and laughed: "*Her-her-her-HER-her!* May I come in? It's a little difficult to walk in these orthopedic shoes." He stepped into the room and, astonishingly, he was wearing enormous black clown shoes about two feet long. "Italy is really the *only* place you can get first-rate shoes." He struck another comic freeze-frame and laughed: "*Her-her-her-HER-her!* Wait! I almost forgot." He slapped his swim-fin feet back to the door, reached around the jamb, and retrieved his banjo. "Somebody left this lying in the hall." He strummed the instrument loudly, leaned against the tiny sink, and sang at full stage-volume:

"I'm a ramblin' guy,
Ramblin' guy, ramblin' guy,
Just a ramblin' guy,
A ramblin' guy,
Ramblin', ramblin', ramblin' guy..."

He stopped dead—then looked at her, confused. "You don't like it? That's 'cause you're not a *ramblin' guy, ramblin' guy, ramblin' guy, ramblin' guy, ramblin' guy.* Now if you were a *ramblin' guy, ramblin' guy, ramblin' guy,* you'd understand I'm just a *ramblin' guy, ramblin' guy....*"

And here, despite her best effort, she laughed. His act was astonishing in its single-minded vaudevillian grotesqueness, all the more alarming as Martin was no longer a young man. She thought: he's Archie Rice in *The Entertainer*; he's every old-timer they'd wheeled onto the stage of the Shrine Auditorium for one last turn; the guy who'd tap-dance, red-faced, for one final standing ovation, then die of a coronary in the wings.

Time, she thought, took a terrible toll on comedians. She remembered Groucho, losing his hair, making that terrible movie with Marilyn Monroe late in his career: pretending to leer, pretending he had the energy of twenty years earlier.

Martin's face was papery and drawn, even slightly skeletal. His eyes were small, guarded, enigmatic—a little desperate.

"*That's* better!" Martin said. "You're finally laughing because underneath it all, you know what? You're just a *ramblin' girl, a ramblin' girl, a ramblin' girl.*"

"Stop, please! I'm going to choke on my water!"

"You're just a *chokin' girl, a chokin' girl, just a chokin' girl.*"

"Stop, please."

"Can I have one of those waters?"

Grafton nodded.

On each of three tiny triangular shelves above the writing desk stood a plastic water bottle. "You'll have to excuse me. I'm rehearsing. I told 'em I'd do a little comedy and magic after dinner. That's what I'm carrying *this* for."

He reached into the pocket of his oversized black sports jacket. *Snap! Yow!* Up came his left hand waving around another oversized mousetrap. He sang out: "*I'm just a cryin' guy, a cryin' guy.*" He painfully extracted his fingers, then reached back in his pocket. He rooted around in there, making an elaborate and complicated show of it. "Hold this a second!" He pulled out a rubber chicken, handed it to her, then rooted around again.

Can't stop performing, Grafton thought.

He wore a heavily starched white shirt buttoned all the way up to his collar, and she thought how uncomfortable he must be on this ancient train with no air conditioning, his pockets loaded with mousetraps and rubber chickens.

"Must be in my *pants* pocket." Here he plunged his hand into his left pocket and went into this elaborate physical routine of a man goosing himself. "Ooooh! Ahhhh! No way! Whooooa!" He swiveled his hip round and round as if he were tearing something loose, and then finally lifted out from his baggy trousers a full-sized sponge-rubber penis with sponge-rubber testicles hanging off the bottom of it. "Damn! I always *do* that! Here, hold this a second."

"I'd rather not."

"No prob!" He folded it up, like a magician crushing a sponge ball, until it fit into his palm, and then he stuffed it into his mouth, where he did a ten-second miming of swallowing. And it was gone. He smacked his lips loudly. "Thank God *that's* over." He looked at his watch. "I figure it'll take about two and a half days to pass through my digestive system. If I time it right, I can produce it outta my ass just in time for the Paris Gay Pride Parade, *her-her-her-HER-her!*" Then he drew from his pocket a long antique-looking pistol with a carved wooden handle.

She thought that for all her writing about guns, the proximity of a real gun in the hands of a stranger was terrifying.

"I hope it's not loaded."

"Oh, it *is* loaded." He aimed the barrel at his own face and did a Three Stooges *nyaah, aaah, aaah.* Then he turned it away. "For my bullet-catching act."

"Your magic show?"

"Some might call it magic," he said in mock-philosophical tones. "Others might call it a feat of preter-natural physical dexterity. William Robinson, performing as the great Chung Ling Soo, was killed doing this one in 1918. Poor bastard took the bullet right in the throat. But, hey, don't you worry, I've been practicing *all afternoon.*"

He took a lavish swig from his water bottle and immediately water streamed out from the hole in his throat—or at least from the top button of his collar which apparently had been gimmicked for that purpose. "Have I got this trick down or what!"

The water was now shooting up into his face.

"Let me borrow your wedding ring," he said.

"What?"

"Lend it to me for just a second. I've got a variation on the linking rings that's going to *blow your mind!"*

She was handing him her ring as someone knocked.

It was Paolo.

"Signor Martin, signora Grafton, I am going to need you pass-a-ports. As we pass through Austria, Germany, Switzerland, and France we need to show the authorities."

"No problem, my good man," said Martin with theatrical brio. He reached into his inner breast pocket and—*snap! yow!*—out came the oversized mousetrap again. "I am *terribly* sorry!" He waved the trap painfully. "I must have left all my papers in mmmm...mmmm..." Something was now stuck in his throat. He mimed it rising up into his mouth, and he pulled a strand of multi-colored tissue from his lips—shrugging his shoulders and shaking his head as if to say: *I don't understand it either.* He pulled on the strand of tissue, and it spooled out from his mouth: one foot, two feet, now a yard. Still he shrugged in embarrassment—both hands now pulling and winding as twenty feet of tissue uncoiled from his lips as fast as he could yank it. As he pulled out the paper streamer he hummed *The Sabre Dance.*

Paolo was laughing, and even Grafton gave up trying to resist.

He was a madman, she thought, but an entertaining madman. With those shrunken raisin eyes. She thought again of Archie Rice. Laurence Olivier in that bowtie and those white gloves. *Look at my eyes. I'm dead behind these eyes.*

She thought: *If he wants to sleep with me, I'm going to let him.* He was just too crazy to resist.

Instructions had been explicit: one had to "dress" for dinner on the Orient Express. As Grafton opened the carriage door into the dining car, she observed that the passengers seemed to fall into two groups: those who looked comfortable in all this opulence, laughing loudly, ordering off the stiff menu boards in Italian—and those, like herself, who looked pathologically shy, terrified of precipitating an international incident through some colossal faux pas with a dessert fork.

She reminded herself to get her wedding ring back later.

Of course, the very sight of food was enough to make her throw up, but this was her birthday trip, and she was to determined to make the best of it. She'd telephone Stephen about it tomorrow when she got to Paris. "It was a once-in-a-lifetime experience," she'd say. "Thank you *so* much." And, truly, *once* was all she could endure of being violently sick on the Orient Express, this rolling symbol of pointless excess. *No wonder half the world hates us,* she thought. She was proud that her fiction was populated by chambermaids and hospital secretaries and nursing-home patients and Spanish cooks and Latino chauffeurs. Her books couldn't afford air conditioning; they ran, on the hottest days, with their windows rolled all the way down, filled with the great hot ache of the working poor. Standing in her absurd heels on that absurd train, she was suddenly proud of her ability to articulate powerlessness.

Equally absurd was the fact that sitting opposite her at the reserved table marked *S. Grafton* was Steve Martin, although this time he was not wearing his clown shoes. He was talking out loud into a miniature tape recorder. "Memo to self: Surprise Sue Grafton at dinn—oh, *hello!*" He put down the recorder. "What a surprise! And what a fantastic coincidence that we're sitting together!"

He really does want to sleep with you, she thought. She was not unpleased.

She noticed a small wrapped present on the table. The wrapping paper had been fashioned from a map of the route of the Orient Express.

"...Mr. Martin," she began.

"Please." He raised a hand in protest. "Not *Mr. Martin.* I want you to call me a *smart facile thinker with a serious reach.*"

She smiled.

"*Variety.* You have to give the attribution or else it's infringement. I think it's true, don't you? *A smart facile thinker with a serious reach.*"

"Look. I'm flattered you want to have dinner with me. But I'm just telling you I don't feel well."

"Of course, *smart, facile*...that's probably redundant, isn't it? I mean, how can you be facile and *not* smart? Right? And *a serious reach*...well, really, what does *that* mean? He's got a serious *reach*? So, like, okay, when my secretary bends over to pick up a pencil I can do a really good Benny Hill?"

"I so appreciate your trying to be funny; it's a wonderful gift you're offering me, but, I have to tell you, I'm just not feeling well."

"Sure!" He held his hands up like *what, me worry?* "You appreciate my trying to be funny. *Trying* to be funny. Not that I *am* funny. I'm just a sad, pathetic clown trying, *albeit unsuccessfully*, to be funny. Look, it's no—"

"Please. I'm not well."

"That's why I love you. Because I'm even *sicker* than you are."

"Let's bring this down a notch, okay? Let's enjoy dinner if we're going to sit together. I don't want to fight with you. I love your work. Like everybody else who's staring at you on this train does. I grew up on your work. But I just want a quiet dinner tonight, okay? You don't have to perform."

"Absolutely," he said. "I appreciate that. You're very kind. You grew up on my work. Exactly. Thirty years ago you thought I was funny. Thirty years ago when I was the wild and crazy guy you thought I was amusing. I made you chuckle once—thirty years ago—in some dorm room where you were getting high, and *Saturday Night Live* was playing in the background. Hey, I appreciate that *once*, during the Jimmy Carter administration, I almost made you smile. That's *very* rewarding."

She smiled at him as warmly as she could. "You're a smart facile thinker with a serious reach."

"*Thinker!* That's the problem! You don't call a playwright a great *thinker*—you call him a great *writer*, okay? You don't say Shakespeare or Chekhov was a great *thinker*, you say he was a magnificent *playwright*, a magnificent *poet*."

"You wanted *Variety* to compare you to Shakespeare?"

He folded his hands and looked at her with tenderness. "Let's talk about *you*."

Grafton smiled.

Martin continued: "And how much *you* love *my* work. Not my recent work! No, no, no, no, no, no, no—my work from *thirty fucking years* ago!" He smashed his fist into the table. The silverware went flying.

Grafton looked at him with affection. He really *was* a broken clown. Hungry for one more laugh. And she *liked* him. She liked the lunatic vulnerability beneath the performance.

"I love *your* work," he said earnestly. He was staring directly at her now. "It's a vision of a world where justice is possible, where honor is rewarded, where mysteries really can be solved."

Apparently, he was serious.

She wasn't sure if he was setting her up for a joke, but she was touched just the same.

"Thank you."

He nodded.

"It's very rare I hear my work analyzed in terms of a world where justice is possible," she said. "Usually, it's 'Boy, your books are a God-send when I've got two hours to kill in the airport.'"

"Oh, that *too*," said Martin. "I read through *A* through *L* while I was taking a dump at O'Hare. I mean, it was a *long* dump. *Her-her-her-HER-her!*"

They were finishing their cups of *camomilla* when the maître d' brought in a tiny chocolate cake, lit with a single candle, and set it before Grafton.

"They weren't serving cake tonight, but I convinced the chef to make it specially for you," said Martin.

"It's not really my birthday."

"I know. That was four months ago."

"You know a lot about me."

"For readers like me, *every* day is your birthday."

"You've really read my books?"

"Every word. I'm in love with Kinsey Millhone."

The crowd in the dining room was smiling and sharing in the moment. She thought they were probably too multi-lingual to sing "Happy Birthday." And how did you get *joyeux anniversaire* to scan to "Happy Birthday" anyway?

Martin put his long pale fingers on hers. "Many happy returns, Susan. I genuinely love the books. I think there's something heroic in them."

"Heroic?"

"For someone like me there is. I'm a comedy writer. I write a sentence and then instantly turn it upside down, search for the pun, look for the way I might ironically reprise it later; it's this whole terrible *lattice*. This *construct*. I look back over those casuals I wrote for *The New Yorker*—that I labored over like they were *Ulysses*—and they seem so hopelessly empty now. Sound and fury and a pointlessness that feels absolutely…depressing. Like a party where no one will shut up. What I admire is that you just *tell the story*. Talk about these characters in a way we know you honestly *believe* in them. And despite all the witty banter with Lieutenant Dolan and that charming old landlord—"

"Henry."

"Right. See? He's got a name. He *exists*. Exists with as much substance as that woman over there." He pointed to a kind of ridiculous-looking American woman in her thirties wearing red cowboy boots, and a red, white, and blue leather vest. She had androgynously short red hair that peeped out of the white cowboy hat she was wearing. Bright red lipstick and a white, pleated skirt. Her dining companion was Big Nigel.

"All those *orphans* you write about so compassionately," continued Martin. "Those alcoholics, those terrible marriages. Those women abused by all those *monsters*. All that yearning for emotional closure. Find my missing mother! Find the name of that poor, anonymous dead girl in the rock quarry! The narratives are like this arrow." He represented an arrow with his finger, and Grafton thought that what was strange and compelling about this speech was that it was being delivered without a shred of irony. "This knife," he continued, "that cuts straight through to the end and brings meaning to everything that came before. That actually restores some sort of psychic balance to the universe.... For someone like me, who spends his time writing jokes, disposable jokes, your work is very touching, and I want to thank you for it."

"I honestly believe you mean that."

"I do. And, I mean, it's so hard to believe in *anything* anymore, you know? Like religion. You can't really take it seriously because it seems so mythological and arbitrary. On the other hand, science is just pure empiricism and, by virtue of its method, excludes metaphysics. I guess I wouldn't believe in *anything* if it weren't for my *Lucky Astrology Mood Watch*."

Grafton had heard the joke before, but she smiled. "And *I* believe that you'll have to eat 90% of this cake because I'm sick to my stomach."

"Folks!" said Martin to the room as he got up. "We've got a wonderful birthday cake here, and we want to share it with all of you!"

For a half-second tears came to her eyes, then just as quickly passed. Martin was on his feet with the cake plate and the silver serving knife. There was something in the work-the-room extravagance of his gestures that reminded her of the other Steve; her husband Steve Hughes. She had begun to think of their relationship as more of good dinner companions than of husband and wife. And, yes, Steve would never hurt her. And, yes, Steve would always be generous. And, yes, his taste in clothing would always be bad; she'd stop him at the door before they left for dinner: "Would you change your shirt?"

He'd get exasperated and say: "Suppose our positions were reversed, and I stopped *you* before we went out and said, 'You're not wearing *that* blouse, are you?'"

"Then I would change it."

"You'd tell me to mind my own damn business."

"You'd never *ask* me to change my blouse."

"Exactly. Because I wouldn't in a million years *presume* to dictate your tastes."

"You wouldn't *have* to because never in a million years would I be wearing a Target-remainder-table Hawaiian shirt."

"This is Land's End. Overstock."

"Overstock! Gee, how on earth could that shirt be overstocked? Maybe because there aren't ten people on the face of the earth with taste so bad they'd buy a shirt with huge purple and green paisleys on it?"

Their arguments were funny and they *weren't* funny.

She'd always felt that she had within her an almost inexhaustible reserve of good humor, optimism, and the irrational belief that things would work out. But, increasingly, that reserve seemed to be emptying. Maybe it was her health problems: those endless urinary infections that appeared sometimes to her as the physical embodiment of death—the voice that said: *Take all the antibiotics you want, Susan. One day I will defeat you. I'm waiting here in the shadows.* It was a voice getting louder and louder, and maybe its presence was making her feel a little reckless.

Maybe part of this trip had been to put her in the path of danger.

She thought that if she only felt a little better she would definitely sleep with Steve Martin. That was kind of alluring in a wild-Sue-Grafton-in-her-twenties way. Kind of crazy and kind of horrifying, too. She imagined that huge nose of his an inch above her face. He'd be howling like a cross-eyed hillbilly: *Her-her-her-HER-her!* All the while she'd be fantasizing about Paolo, and Martin would be fantasizing about Claire Danes.

That's my weakness, Grafton thought. Too quick to call judgment down on everybody else, and too blind and too suffocatingly vain to call down any serious judgment on myself. Ms. Austen had framed it nimbly: *For what do we live but to make sport for our neighbors, and laugh at them in our turn?* Wry Jane. The merry spinster. Dead at 41. Remembered by the world as a remarkable mind. And how would the world remember Sue Grafton? *M is for Mediocre? P is for Past Her Prime?*

"I want to give you a present," said Martin. He handed her the small package wrapped in a map. He was smiling, earnest, eager. "Of course, I had to throw it together at the last second. I didn't know you were going to be on this train. If I had known ahead of time, I would have steamed off the remainder sticker."

She unwrapped the map to reveal a paperback copy of *Picasso at the Lapin Agile and Other Plays* by Steve Martin. On the front cover was a red sticker from Barnes & Noble that said *Formerly $12–Now $.99*

"You just *can't* get those stickers off," he said. "Believe me, I tried. I had it soaking in the bidet for the last hour."

"This looks wonderful. I'm very flattered."

"I signed it for you."

On the title page he had written: *Boldly and warmly inscribed by the author.*

She smiled.

"These are the best things I ever wrote," said Martin. "And this is the best line. It's said by the Girl." Looking at Grafton with complete seriousness, he recited from memory: *"Everything you said and did, every touch at night in bed, every act of kindness, every generosity, every loving comment had this sentence attached: Maybe now she'll love me."*

There was a pause, then she threw up all over him.

Midnight.

Maybe the train was still in Austria.

She remembered Innsbruck, Landeck, Saint Ainton, Bludenz, Feldkirch—then the sky darkened and the noise of the train intensified and the names of the cities started sounding, to her ears, like concentration camps: Buchs, Rorschech, Winterthur.

The train came to a dead stop. She looked out the window at a station sign that might have read Basel, and it was hard to shake the image of the camps. The jackboots marching through the train cars. Maybe it was two a.m. She was green. Truly green, lying in her fold-down bed, bathed in sweat, her stink filling the small compartment, penetrating the upholstery. This is the car where Sue Grafton died. We had to lock it up because we just couldn't get rid of the smell.

She had tried to call Stephen Hughes on a borrowed cell phone, but there was no signal in Basel. *Host lost* read the phone.

Christ, the diarrhea again!

She hoisted herself out of bed in her navy nightshirt with a yellow Rat Fink stenciled on it. Barefoot, she thumped down the carpeted corridor. She passed in the flashing streaks of light—the train was moving again—the woman in the red cowboy boots and the red, white, and blue leather vest. What on earth was she doing up at this hour? And completely dressed? Maybe she really *was* a hooker, and she was working her way down the car. Or she'd gotten up to floss her teeth. *Floss! Floss! The memory comes—along those remote beaches, over the glossy evening sands of the past....*

Everything she'd ever read was locked somewhere in her head. Touch a neuron, Doctor, and out it pours. Everything locked in that tiny, tragic skull. She was going to throw up again. No, she wasn't. The Goddamn bathroom door was locked. Somebody in there. She stood in the darkness. Considered knocking. Please open up. I'm in trouble here. One more minute and I'm going to shit all over my legs. She'd worked in a nursing home in her twenties, and she could still see her first day on the job: a poor elderly woman in a cantaloupe-colored night shirt standing in the lobby, listening to a nurse, and suddenly the elderly woman took a shit just standing there talking. It dropped messily to the ground like mustard-streaked wet sand, and the nurse cried out: "Oh, Abigail, look what you've done! Susan, see if you can get this cleaned up." It was forty years later and still she saw it: mustard-streaked wet sand, half on the floor, half on Abigail's fragile ankle.

The bathroom door was finally opened.

The guy with the khaki shirt and the aluminum attaché case.

The light switch above the door; the lock, an old-fashioned silver hook-and-eye on the bottom of the door.

She looked at herself in the mirror: ghastly, green, gaunt—birthday girl—hair streaked with sweat. *Oh, Abigail, look what you've done!* She wanted to cry...that illness could make you this *small*. It was those damn mussels in Venice, in that terrible green sauce, aspic like green spittle, like Nyquil. She was going to throw up again. She went down on her bare knees and clutched the sides of the toilet bowl.

Nothing.

Just this headache crawling now over the left side of her face. She rinsed her hands and tried to gag herself into throwing up. She coughed and choked but nothing arose.

She sat on the toilet and drank three consecutive paper cups of water. Her stomach was seething—uncoiling like a serpent. Then came the blast again: a nightmare shit-storm. She closed her eyes and moaned in anguish.

She flushed the toilet instantly; she couldn't bear to see the effluvia. Her face was sweating again. What happened to waste on a train? Did it just fly out over the dark rails of Switzerland? Heidi and Helmut, quietly fornicating on the side of the tracks in the healthy Alpine night, are suddenly showered with American diarrhea?

Then there was a knock on the door. A female voice with a French accent: "Is everything all right?"

"I'll be out in a minute."

She flushed the toilet again. Out in the darkness Helmut got another icy manure bath: *Gottdamnit, not again!*

"I'm not feeling very well."

Grafton staggered back through the corridor: seasick, drunk. The train suddenly stopped. Then it seemed to go in reverse even faster and noisier than before. There was a shouting of voices in German. Grafton looked out and saw a sign that might have read: *Meichtal.*

God only knew where they were.

Room 3482 was beginning to feel like hell. There was no escape from the terrible rhythm of the tracks. The room was a sweatbox and to open the window was to invite inside the noise of a construction site. She took another capful of the Pepto-Bismol she'd brought, spilled more of it on her navy Rat Fink nightshirt, and fell into bed. Immediately she had to move her bowels again.

She steadied herself against it, turned to the tiny nightlight, tried to read *Madame Bovary.*

They thought she was delirious, and from midnight on she was: brain fever had set in.... Sometimes her heart would pain her, then it would be her chest, her head or her limbs; she had fits of vomiting....

Grafton put down the novel. *Brain fever!*

Her stomach was churning; she could audibly hear the valves opening inside her, the chambers filling with poison....

Then she was running down the corridor again.

She passed Steve Martin coming the other way; he was still completely dressed, wearing those enormous shoes.

He's performing.

"What are you do—"

"I'm sick!" she said. "Out of the way, please!"

Then she was locking the silver hook-and-eye on the bottom of the bathroom door, and she practically fell into the toilet before she realized the seat wasn't down.

The serpents were sliding again. Turning and arching. A massive release of gas. Then a log-jam of the large intestine.

No more paper cups.

She held her forehead in her hands, moved to get up, and then sat down again as the wet sickness poured out of her.

"God have mercy."

Now the train seemed to stop again. Outside, in the darkness, a sign read: *Meiringen.*

She washed up. She was desperate to take a shower, but there was nowhere to do that on the train.

Why had she eaten that chocolate cake?

Bells sounded from a distant train station.

The bells are Meiringen, she thought.

Back at her room Steve Martin stood waiting for her.

"Do you want me to tell the conductor?" he asked seriously. "Maybe we need to get you to a hospital."

"No, I'm all right."

He produced a bottle of water. "You have to keep drinking so you don't dehydrate."

"Thank you. I'm drinking, I'm drinking."

"Some birthday?"

"Yes, I'm sure it's just what my husband dreamed of when he bought me this ticket."

"Let me help you."

"Thank you. Really. But go back to bed."

"Just let me make sure you're all right."

"I need to sleep."

"At least it's a birthday you won't forget."

Martin gently ushered her back into her room.

"My real birthday is April 24th. But I had a urinary infection on April 24th."

"*April 24th.* You know what I hear in my head when you say that? I had a record when I was a kid. Caedmon Records, do you remember those? With the green and white labels? Basil Rathbone reading Sherlock Holmes. I played it over and over. The way you do when you're a kid. The way you *imbibe* stuff. And I can still hear Basil Rathbone." Here Martin did an impressive bit of mimicry. "*It was with no surprise, therefore, that I saw him walk into my consulting-room upon the evening of April 24th."*

The train lurched to a stop. The electric lights suddenly extinguished, and the train was in total darkness.

She could hear a scuffling in the corridor—voices shouting in German. She lay on her back frozen in both terror and in the hopelessness of illness. *The camps,* she thought. The jackboots on the train. The SS guards.

And now there really *were* jackboots in the hallway. Louder now—and approaching.

"Oh, Christ," she said out loud, and she held onto the side of her tiny bed.

"Don't worry," whispered Martin. "This is what you wanted."

She felt his hand on her forearm. But then she smelled alcohol and the inside of her elbow was being swabbed and then there came what must have been the pin-prick of a needle.

"Stephen!" she cried out, and she wondered in that last terrible second if it was a cry to her husband or to Steve Martin.

Her arm was turning to ice when she heard the door to her room being kicked in.

Lethal Injection, she thought.

Good title.

TWO

BNGRBRNT

The page-proof in front of him read: *Praise for the Work of Stephen King*. With red pen he changed "praise" to "raves." Then he underlined "Stephen King" twice and wrote in the margin: *All caps and add exclamation point*.

There were quotations down the page from *The New York Times Book Review, The Wall Street Journal, Publisher's Weekly, Playboy, Time, Esquire,* and *People*.

He wrote on the bottom of the page: *Add attached blurbs*. Then he stapled to the proofs four completely filled typewritten sheets of quotations: *The Palm Beach Post, Interview,* Michael Connelly ("Top shelf. You couldn't go wrong with a King book."), Mordecai Richler, *Chattanooga Times, Flint Journal, Baton Rouge Advocate….* He'd spent all night going through his files ("Stephen King is the Winslow Homer of blood"—*The New Yorker*.)

A few weeks ago, he'd cleaned up a sort of bastard novella and shipped it off to Posthumous Press to be published as a paperback original, and he was determined to send off this conspicuously second-rate manuscript ("Top shelf!") with as much critical bombast as he could muster. It was like that song that Tabitha loved to play in the car: *Long as you keep 'em way off balance/How can they spot you got no talents?*

"Stephen," she'd said to him, "it doesn't matter what you send them. You can send them a piece of used toilet paper and they'd publish it. Don't worry about it. Let's take the money and run. It's another vacation."

She was right, of course, but the used toilet paper crack stuck in his throat. And, finally, in a gesture that might politely be called self-destructive, he retitled the novella *Stool Sample.*

"Great title," wrote Jerry Goniff at Posthumous. "Both witty, ironic, and intriguing."

Terrific, King thought. *Both* followed by three adjectives. *I've got morons on my team.* He was getting published by a functional illiterate who probably hadn't even read what he'd sent him. *Christ, we got something by Stephen King. Take out a full-page ad in PW.*

He wondered what the slug-line would be:
Stool Sample: Take the plunge!
Stool Sample: Overflowing with excitement!
Stool Sample: A bowlful of terror!

No one read anymore anyway. What the hell did it matter? People bought those 40-page gag books by the cash register. *Inside the Mind of George W. Bush.* Blank book, haha.

He walked to the computer and opened the page he'd bookmarked: Amazon Books. *Lisey's Story* by Stephen King. He scrolled down. Amazon Sales Ranking: 246. "Fuck," he said aloud. Yesterday's sales ranking: 204. It was getting worse. How could a Stephen King novel already be up to 246? In six months? He was Stephen King! He'd been on the cover of *Newsweek* for fuck's sake! He used to stay on the best-seller list for a year. He had the #1 book ten Christmases in a row! Now his books stayed on the list for three weeks before they were relegated to the $1.99 pile. Pretty soon they'd be remaindering his books six months *before* publication.

Did he hear something?

"Tabitha?"

No answer.

He suddenly visualized her hanging dead in the kitchen. Naked. Hanging from an extension cord. A note around her neck: *Your next.* (Killers never *did* get the grammar right.) The phone lines were already cut: they'd pulled the main line out of the interface box.

Another noise downstairs.

"Tabby?"

Maybe it was Pluto, his black cat.

The alarm box glowed green—all 72 contact-switches undisturbed, circuits closed, all doors and windows sealed tight. Of course, one six-inch piece of wire with two alligator clips in the attic could bypass the entire alarm—close the circuit in a loop and render every door and window vulnerable. They'd set it all up earlier in the week when "Supreme Security" had come for their yearly replacement of the power-failure battery. Complete access to the house. "Good to see you again, Mr. King." Now please stay out of our way while we short-circuit your entire system so later this week my associates can rob you blind while they torture you.

Something suspicious about the woman they sent, too: slightly overweight, red-faced, in her twenties. Since when did women do this kind of work—creeping around hot attics, stepping onto the support timbers between the old fiberglass insulation—a tool belt, a blue bandana, and a barbed-wire tattoo? The perfect diversion really. Send a young woman to give him a hot blue-eyed look that said: Come on, let's fool around on the fiberglass, Stephen, and then fall through the ceiling onto your dining room table. Hey, Mr. World's Best Selling Novelist, let me make your Amazon sales ranking climb.

He should have written down her name and then called Supreme Security to see if anybody named "Jane" really worked there.

"Jane? Sure. She worked here about three years ago. Up until…"

"Up until what?"

"Well, we never really could *prove* anything, Mr. King."

There was a soft thumping now from upstairs. Somebody walking barefoot.

"Tabby?"

The kitchen should have been well lit that afternoon, but the criss-cross bars over all the windows cast a network of shadows against the clay-colored Spanish tiles on the floor and walls.

He punched S-P-R-U-C-E (Tabby's maiden name) into the alarm control hidden in the kitchen closet. An amber light illuminated as around the house 14 infrared heat and motion detectors glowed deep crimson in the walls. These were the satanic eyes of his house.

"Okay, asshole," he said to his invisible intruder. "Just try to walk around now."

He strained to listen.

Other than the humming of the refrigerator there was no noise.

The silence began scaring him so he turned on the battery radio he kept in case of power outages. John Fogerty's voice blasted out at full volume, rattling the radio's cheap plastic case.

It ain't me, it ain't me,
I ain't no millionaire's son!

King sang along with the radio. *"I ain't no fortunate one!"*

The radio, like every other radio in the house, was tuned to WKIT-FM, the classic rock station that King himself had purchased when it was about to go bankrupt. Now it existed thanks to a few local sponsors but mostly due to his own largesse. *Large Ass*—a novel by Tabitha King. Okay, that was cruel. "Cancel, cancel," he said out loud. All women in middle age had big asses. Even the ones on the treadmills.

Tabitha had asked him the other month: "Stephen, I was trying to go back through the history of my searches on the computer, and it said *teen bikini.* Were you looking up pictures of teen bikinis? You're not secretly a child molester, are you? I didn't mean to look, but it came up under the search histories."

And he thought: What am I supposed to look up when I want to find dirty pictures? *Middle-aged female bowlers in sweatpants? Hysterectomy Hotties?* He said: "I was looking up a possible graphic for the television series."

"I think you're turning into Dirty Bird Joe."

"No, no, the series on TNT: *Stephen King's The Best of Stephen King: Selected by Stephen King and Introduced by the Author.*" He thought a second. "Do you think I should change the *Author* to *Stephen King?* I want to make sure people know who's responsible."

The phone was ringing in the office. He moved into the hall and immediately the alarms started screaming. It was loud enough to give an intruder a coronary. The sirens were located in the attic where they blasted out through the air vents. The entire house was shaking.

Now the private phone line in the kitchen was also ringing. "Hold on a second, for Christ's sake." He punched in the code to turn off the infrared sensors, and he picked up the phone as the sirens went silent.

"Supreme Security, do you require assistance?"

"No, I accidentally set off the alarm. Everything's fine here."

"We need the password."

"*Over 40 Million King Books in Print.*"

"That is incorrect."

"Oh, right. I updated it. *Over 47 Million King Books in Print.*"

"Thank you."

He moved towards the "public" phone in the office. The caller ID box read *Bangor Daily News.* He let the answering machine respond. On his outgoing message there was the sound of wind, rain, and spooky laughter which he had dubbed off his old 33 r.p.m. record of *Walt Disney Presents the Thrilling, Chilling Sounds of the Haunted House*—an album he had bought for 79 cents when he was sixteen years old. "This is Stephen King. Thank you for calling Dial-a-Curse," announced his voice on the tape. "In dialing the seven digits of this number, you have cast an ancient and irretrievable curse on yourself and your family. You will die within ten days of making this call. If you would like to die in an automobile accident, please press one. If you would like your child to die instead of you, please press the pound key. If you would like to leave a message, please do so after the tone, although hearing the tone means you have also cursed your first-born."

Beep.

"Mr. King, this is Renee Shih-THAY-add, calling from the *Bangor Daily News.* I'm the news editor, and we wanted to see if we could get a quotation from you about the death of Sue Grafton. You can call me at 990-8138 or e-mail me at R. Shih-Thay-Add at bangordailynews.com. That's R-S-H-I...T-H...E-A-D at—"

He picked up the phone. "You spell your name *Shithead?*"

She spoke carefully: cultured, clipped tones with an accent that might have been Jamaican. "It's pronounced shih-THAY-add. It's French. My family is Haitian. They're very proud of their name."

"It must have been tough going to school with a name like that."

"People got used to it. Now, I'm calling about the death of—"

"But that first day? When they read your name off the roll? *Shithead, Renee.* God, to endure twelve years of that."

"People were sensitive to it."

"I can't believe your parents would subject you to that."

"Mr. King, my parents are proud of their name. As I said, I am calling about the death of Sue Grafton, whose body turned up this morning in Switzerland."

"Renee Shithead."

"Shih-THAY-add."

"*Shih-thay-add.* Do you think there are people running around named, I don't know, Clarence Fuckwad? Or Vicki Sue Vaginabreath?"

"Sue Grafton is what this call's about. We thought, as a famous writer, you might give us a quote, a local hook so we're not just running the wire service."

"Francesca Sportsbra, I want you to meet Terrence Bloated-Scrotum. And this is his beautiful daughter Rebecca Fecal-Smear."

"Mr. King—"

"It's Kin-*Guh.* Two syllables. My family were morons and very proud of the fact."

"*What?*"

"I said they were Mormons and very proud of the fact. Okay. Quote. You ready?"

"This'll be great. I'm ready. This is terrific. To have a bestselling author of one genre commenting on a bestselling author in another—"

"Whoa! Hold it right there. You're going to identify me as a *genre* writer? Did I hear you correctly?"

"I'll identify you anyway you—"

"Did you read my acceptance speech for the National Book Foundation's Medal for *Distinguished Service to American Letters*? Did you read my speech? Do you even know I won it? And, listen, that's Distinguished Service to American Letters, not Distinguished Service to Dumb Fucks who Want to Read a Book Where a Guy's Head Explodes. Okay? Are you still there?"

"I'm here."

"Well, listen. You want to learn something? Go on Amazon and order the CD of my acceptance speech. It's got an Amazon Sales Ranking of 146,279 because the dumb fucks who read my books didn't even know I won it. And this is the *same* award that John Updike won, all right? And Arthur Fucking Miller. Death of a Fucking Salesman! Okay, so why do they give it to me?"

"Mr. King—"

"Did they give it to me 'cause I'm a *horror* writer, a *genre* writer? The guy who wrote *Tales from the Crypt*? No, they gave it to Stephen Fucking King because I'm a *real* writer, okay?"

"I never said—"

"I've written essays. Did you ever read *Danse Macabre*? That's Goddamn *literary* criticism, lady. And did you read my *New Yorker* stuff on Little League baseball? Okay? When they need a Halloween story for *The New Yorker* they don't call up J.D. Fucking Salinger, they call up Stephen King. So you can take your little *Bangor Daily News* hook—one genre writer commenting on another—and you can shove it up your—"

She hung up.

"Fuck you," said King.

It sounded as if a chair fell somewhere. There was definitely someone in the house.

"Hello! Is there anybody there?" he called out, and he immediately thought how stupid that was. If he'd been watching a grade-C horror movie on television and the hero, alone in the house, had called out: "Hello! Is there anybody there?" King would have spoken back to the television: "Yeah, it's me. The fucking serial killer in my Ben Cooper Spooktown skeleton mask. I'm hiding in the upstairs bathroom behind the shower curtain. I like the smell of your coconut conditioner. Is there anything else you want to know? The security code on my VISA? It's 2-5-8."

"Tabby!" he called out, and the name caught in his throat.

She was gone. After 35 years of marriage she had finally walked: all the private language of a lifetime and the hotel rooms shared in Charlottesville at the Virginia Festival of the Book....

He sat at the kitchen table and poured himself a glass of Walnut Acres organic concord grape juice because even though he wouldn't permit himself to drink wine anymore, it sort of *tasted* like wine. He could convince himself it was wine.

WKIT-FM was playing "Midnight Rambler" or some other piece-of-shit Allman Brothers song. They were always playing the wrong song. He dialed the jock. "Hey, can you play some John Fogerty?"

"Are you listening, dude? I just played some."

"This is Stephen King."

"Okay, man, no problem. And, hey man, I loved *The Colorado Kid.*"

King hung up. "Yeah, sure you did, you lying piece of shit." Even King himself knew that story was dreadful.

Mid-song, the Allman Brothers dissolved into the electronic baseball-stadium-rave-up clapping that began John Fogerty's "Centerfield."

"Excellent," said King. This was exactly the song he needed.

Put me in, coach,
I'm ready to play!

Damnit, he *was* ready to play. *A moment in the sun.* The sound effect of the crack of a bat.

He closed his eyes. He had wanted to be *so* much; he had wanted to be so many people: a significant man of letters, a force to be reckoned with, a man whose life had, in some tiny way, shaped the course of events, even changed the world in some deep-rooted cultural way—so that when they wrote the history of the end of the 20th century, *his* name might be a blip, a footnote, a plaque on the door: *Author Stephen King Lived and Wrote in this House....* Yeah, right. The truth was that Tabitha and his three children would sell this thing so fast—*Motivated Seller*, the realty sign would read—in other words, *Can't Get Rid of This Drafty Overpriced Piece of Shit.* And the *Bangor Daily News* will interview Tabitha about the sale: "Frankly, I couldn't wait to get rid of it. The memories, the history—good and bad—it was like a prison cell."

Put me in, coach!

He caught sight of himself in the dark, rippled reflection of the oven door.

A cry rose from his chest.

He removed his pink seersucker shirt and looked at himself in the oven door. He was the Biafra poster boy. *Rib-eye Joe,* Tabitha had called him.

He'd had a life. June of 1999 he'd had a life: a family, three grandchildren, ten thousand ideas—and then one walk, one stupid walk on Rt. 5 and Bryan Fucking Smith in his fucking Dodge truck is looking away from the road to reprimand his fucking dog—he isn't watching the road for five fucking seconds—and poor stupid Stephen King is slammed like a manikin off the bumper of his truck.

One second of sloppiness and all life alters.

His body still looked distorted—a smashed marionette poorly reassembled. His face was drawn. The muscles in his leg never unclenched. And this locked muscle in his neck and shoulder. He'd explained it to Tabitha and 1,000 doctors: It's like when you have a crick in your neck and shoulder and you move it and it pops? Well, this one *never* pops. It just pulls and tightens. When it was really bad his left shoulder blade felt as if it were made of iron, and the two lateral muscles in his neck knotted like superballs. Then the spiders started walking across his scalp.

Sometimes he attached an alpha-wave inducer to his earlobes and let it pulse for an hour or he wore a blue HoMedics magnetic band around his neck or a Thermoskin neck sheath at night to keep the muscles warm. He did Alexander Technique; he did acupuncture. Now they wanted him to try a decompression machine to yank his head from his shoulders with fifty pounds of pressure (for $3,000), and all because Bryan Fucking Smith was talking to his dog.

He had really thought about having Smith killed. Oh, that was the call he had wanted to receive from the *Bangor Daily News*: "Mr. King, this is Renee Shithead; did you hear that the driver who struck you, Bryan Smith, was found dead today?"

"My God. Are you kidding me? I hadn't heard anything about it."

"The coroner says his penis was cut off, covered with meat-sauce and served to his rottweiler."

"Astonishing."

"Yes, and then two 12-inch metal spikes were driven through his neck."

"My God, we live in a sick world."

"And the body, still half-alive, was locked into his basement with his rottweiler and, after approximately one week, the dog ate him. The only thing the police could find was a hardback copy of *Bag of Bones* in the skeleton's hands inscribed: *I hope Satan will forgive you because I never will. —S.K.* Any comment?"

"A terrible tragedy for the entire State of Maine. *Maine: The way life should be.*"

Oh, he could have gotten 10,000 lawyers to go after that asshole. Ten thousand lawyers with 10,000 hard-ons had called his office just begging to prosecute *pro-bono* ("pro-boner," as Tabitha had said) for the chance of making themselves famous. But, *noooo*, the Bard of Bangor was going to take the *high* road, the newspapers reported, and let the local District Attorney handle the case: Six months *suspended sentence* for "driving to endanger"! One year's suspension of his license. That's all!

For over a year King had imagined that Smith was out there every morning; waiting with his cane and his dog and that Goddamn space between his teeth; waiting in a station wagon on top of West Broadway; waiting with binoculars, watching King's driveway. "This time I'm gonna *rilly* kill the muthafuckah, hyuh, hyuh, hyuh. Ain't that right, Bullet?" *Ruff! Ruff!*

Then the call had come from CNN in the fall of 2000 that Bryan Smith, age 43, had died at home of "unknown reasons." But even Smith's death had not set King's mind at ease. The irrational rage endured, and the consequences of his injuries endured.

King spoke aloud to the empty kitchen. "And here, gentle reader, is the genuinely unbearable part. Since his accident, Mr. Stephen King can no longer have sex with his wife. Or anyone else for that matter. Including a photograph of a teen bikini."

There. He had said it. His terrible and cosmically insignificant truth thrust out into the world. What had John Updike written? (He was the King of Cock Contemplation but, okay, he occasionally got off a good line.) Updike had been describing his pages of writing: *Why do I produce them but to thrust, by some subjective photosynthesis, my guilt into Nature, where there is no guilt?*

Yes, Updike was an excellent choice for the National Book Foundation's Medal for Distinguished Service to American Letters. Of course, Updike had never written a 526-page novel about a haunted 1958 Plymouth that drove around killing people, but, hell, *Terrorist* was a start! At least it was a sort of Goddamn thriller.... Christ, if Updike wrote a book with a recognizable *plot* in it, the National Book Foundation would have to take back their medal: "Sorry, John, we're giving it to Cormac McCarthy's new book, *Blood on the Blood*. Have you seen it? It's a 1,300-page novel consisting of one sentence. Now *that's* fucking poetry!"

Bitter Joe, Tabitha called him.

Here's Bitter Joe,

He's a-movin' kinda slow...

Tabitha had also claimed that his impotence was not the reason she was *taking some space....*

"You're turning into Reclusive Joe," she said. "You won't go anywhere, and the books are getting worse for it, Stephen. You open your mail with latex gloves. Come on, Stephen, that's sick."

"Hey, Dr. Brown gave me a gross of them. I'm just trying to—"

"It's sick, Stephen. I'm telling you this because I love you."

She'd stood in the kitchen, unable to meet his eyes, ringlets of her still beautiful brown hair falling around her full face.

The car he'd bought for a toy, a 1964 Cadillac hearse, had a license plate which read BNGRBRNT. It was meant as a love letter to Tabby: his Bangor Brunette, but when he saw it these days, it spoke in his ear: Bangor Burnout….

He'd bought the *Sports Illustrated* swimsuit issue hoping it might fan the flame of his fast-extinguishing manhood. He might as well have been staring at the Abu Ghraib atrocity photos. *Brooklyn Decker, Age 18, Born Middleton, Ohio, but raised in Charlotte. I LIVE FOR: "…the fact that millions of old guys, whom I would never even say hello to, are wildly whacking off over my purple polka-dot bikini. That just makes my parents so proud."*

Dr. David Brown had said it was a psychological trauma and not a physiological one. "Your appetite will return," he'd said, smiling.

King had smiled back—the smile of the hopelessly doomed.

No wonder he was looking up teen bikinis on Google….

Tabitha insisted that sex was not her principal disappointment. "I would love to just hug you, Stevie, but you don't even want to do that. You're turning away from me; I can *physically* feel it."

What *did* he want?

He wanted Brooklyn Decker, age 18, to show up unannounced at his door in a bathrobe.

God, he was falling apart.

He moved into the den. There was the paperback of *Madame Bovary* he was forcing himself to read for the men's book club. He had lost his first copy—probably left it at the physical therapist's office. This was his new one: untouched, unread. He read a paragraph at random:

…forehead covered beads of cold sweat…wild eyes and those clutching arms…the presence of something mad, shadowy, and ominous…

Another noise from upstairs.

Oh, come on and kill me already. He shut his eyes. *Kill me and get it over with. What can you really do anyway? The work endures.*

Pathetic writers like Stephen King with his dirty eyeglasses and his sore neck pumped full of trigger-point injections were thrown into boxes and buried deep in the ground like nuclear waste. But their work endured.

He needed a project.

The project would make him sane; it would restore his soul; it would bring Tabitha back to him….

The phone rang. The caller ID read: *New York Times.*

A comment on the death of Sue Grafton as a sidebar to the tribute piece being written by Janet Evanovich for the *Book Review?*

Certainly.

"You know," said King. "Before I improvise a eulogy, I'm not sure of the details of her death."

"No one is," said the male editor. "She's onboard an essentially non-stop train going from Venice to Paris. The trip was some sort of late birthday present. At least three passengers claim that she was in the company of a white-haired guy; *two* of those passengers say he was the comedian Steve Martin, although there is no record of any passenger named Steve Martin on the train. A representative for the real Steve Martin says he was nowhere near the Orient Express."

"Did somebody who looked like Steve Martin get off the train?"

"Not that anyone remembers. What everybody remembers is that Grafton was sick that night. Apparently went to the bathroom all night long. Anyway, the train pulls into *Gare de l'Est* at about 11 a.m., and everybody's been given back his passport—everybody except Grafton. Her carriage is empty. They figure, okay, she's sick. She's in the bathroom. They don't want to embarrass her. But, no, she's gone. Never picked up her passport. Gone. And the train has made no scheduled stops during the night."

"How about unscheduled stops?"

"Not according to the Venice Simplon Orient-Express."

"And her body?"

"The next day, Sunday, two hikers are wandering around the mountains outside Meiringen—"

"Switzerland."

"Up by Interlaken; I have it on a map here; by the Brienzer Sea. These two guys in lederhosen and walking sticks are doing whatever grown men in lederhosen and walking sticks do up there, and they see, right by the waterfall, one of those little alphabetical address books. And written there, right on the first page is *Property of Sue Grafton*, with her addresses in both Kentucky and California. And the book is blank."

"A blank address book?"

"Entirely. Not a single address in there. And under S there's a message left for her husband Stephen."

"*Another* Stephen?"

"What?"

"Nothing," said King. "Just thinking out loud. *C is for Conspiracy.* What did the note say?"

"Husband does not want to reveal the contents. Although a Swiss detective I spoke to who actually saw it told me it was no longer than three lines. And the last line was: *Don't forget to feed the cats.*"

"Jesus, that's the last thing on her mind? Did they find her body?"

"Mangled. At the bottom of the falls. Wedding ring still on."

"What was she doing at the waterfall?"

"No one knows. The train doesn't stop anywhere near Reichenbach Falls. How about that quote?"

"Okay." He stared out the bars of the kitchen window. There was a brown rabbit on the lawn. "Sue Grafton reinvented the modern detective novel. She brought to it a hipness, a snarkiness, a working-class sensibility that defined what we think of as the modern female private detective. She was one of a kind. Absolutely irreplaceable. *G is for Grief....* Please give the attribution as Stephen King, whose recent acceptance speech of the National Book Foundation's Medal for Distinguished Service to American Letters is available as a compact disk on Amazon."

"I don't know if I can fit all that in."

"Try."

"Okay. I love the *G is for Grief* bit. Maybe we can use that as the head."

"Make sure you run the 'absolutely irreplaceable' part."

"By the way, I heard Putnam's already casting around for another writer to keep the series going. Is that something you'd ever be willing to try?"

"I'd consider it an honor."

King found his copy of *The Annotated Sherlock Holmes* and reread "The Final Problem" and its memorable description of Reichenbach Falls:

It is, indeed, a fearful place. The torrent, swollen by the melting snow, plunges into a tremendous abyss, from which the spray rolls up like the smoke from a burning house.

Sherlock Holmes and Professor Moriarty had fallen into that "tremendous abyss," and now, apparently, so had poor Sue Grafton.

But how?

On a train that stopped nowhere near Reichenbach Falls?

Some old voice was speaking to him now. Some old door was creaking open, and outside, in the blue blasting sunlight there stood—and he recognized it in one second—a story idea.

He, Stephen King, would solve the mystery.

Then he would make it into the best Goddamn novel he ever wrote.

"Wow," he said aloud.

Put me in, coach, I'm ready to play.

Madame Danielle Schuelein-Steel Lazard Zugelder Toth Treina y Perkins was not pleased. First, she was not pleased that her name was so long. She had been married five times, and although she did not regret a single minute of any one of those marriages, the list *was* beginning to look suspiciously long—particularly as she was not married at the moment. The world would think—what?—she was *capricious*? She was desperately needy? She was weak?

The thought made her laugh. She was Danielle Schulein: the New York City Jew with the sneakers, the pigtails, the bony shoulders, and the micro-mini. The girl who'd gone from secretarial work for Supergirls to recreating herself as the most popular novelist in the history of American publishing: Danielle Steel. The word *steel* always appealed to her, sounded strong on her tongue. *Steel* was the cloak she wore to the world, and it served her well. Right now it had drawn both the concierge, Georges, and the room-service manager up to her second-floor suite at the Ritz.

"Madame Steel, I am deeply sorry—"

"Sorry doesn't cut it," announced Steel from her throne of pillows on the bed. "As Georges can tell you, I have been coming to the Ritz since 1957 when my father used to bring me here as a child. I have spent *hundreds* of thousands of dollars here."

"Madame, please, you will—"

"And this morning I order some fruit for the room, for my friends. And in addition to being served lousy, second-rate fruit—look! Look at those apples. Look at those grapes. This is the Ritz? This is the world's greatest hotel? So in addition to the second-rate fruit, I am charged...." Here she paused dramatically to look again at the room-service bill. "One hundred and fifty-five euros!"

"Madame Steel," said the manager, who was bowing so low his face was no longer visible. "It is an outrage. A terrible mistake. You should *never* have been billed for this. I hope you will accept—"

"I have been coming here since 1957!"

"Madame Steel, you will allow me to tear up the bill? Please you will allow me?"

She handed him the bill. "And you'll get me some decent fruit? I want some nuts, too, and some cheese, and those little chocolate squares from La Maison du Chocolat."

"*Immediately*, Madame Steel."

"And, Georges?"

"Yes, Madame Steel, what can I do for you?"

"Ah!" said Steel, turning to Curtis, a somewhat overly-intense-looking woman in her late twenties who was there to interview Steel for *Poets and Writers*. "That is what I like—people asking me 'What can I do for you, Danielle?' Because it's *always* the other way around. Can you get me an agent? Can you get me a publisher? Can you get me a deal on Coco Chanel boots? Can you get me a reservation at La Coupole? What I like is: 'What can I do for *you*, Danielle?'"

Curtis dutifully wrote this down in the black hidebound journal she was never without.

"Just name me your wish," said Georges. His tone was both humorous and genuinely affectionate.

"First..." said Danielle, and for a small dark-haired figure on that enormous bed she could hold the room with the sheer power of her presence. "…The CD player is broken. I can't get the Goddamn disk to come out. We were listening to the audiobook of *Toxic Bachelors*: unabridged, 12 CDs read by yours truly, a nightmare to record; we did it last summer in Montecatini. My God, it must have been 90 *degrees* in that studio, but, you know, I'm an artist, I *used* the exhaustion. We were nominated for a Golden Headphone Award; we lost to Judy Kaye reading *Y is for Yidl Mitn Fidl*, can you believe that? A mystery! We lost to a *series* book! *Unbelievable.*"

"Did you hear she killed herself?" asked Curtis.

"Sweet Pea, you're *biting* your soup again. You don't eat soup with your teeth. You use your lips."

Curtis dutifully tried to correct herself.

"Of course I heard she killed herself. Listen, Sweet Pea, whom do you think they *called* for a comment? I told the *International Herald Tribune* that 'the world of letters has lost its greatest practitioner.' Now I choose my words very carefully. I had prepared myself for the call. World of *letters*, do you get it? Because of her alphabet mysteries? So the retard they have working as a copy editor changes it to 'the world of *literature* has lost its greatest practitioner.' The world of literature! Oh, my God, I sounded like *such* a moron. Like Sue Grafton is up there with, like, you know, Mitch Albom? And, listen, *any* death is a loss to me. I mean that." She touched her chest. "As Victor Hugo said—and I want to take you over to his house later in the Place des Vosges—my God, you feel like you've stepped *right* into history, and there's a bakery across the street that makes a raspberry Danish you could *die* for; anyway, as Victor Hugo said: 'No man kills the thing he loves. Every man's death diminishes the island. Every death is a piece of the clod.' I grieve her loss *terribly*, but at the same time my compulsion for brutal honesty forces me to confess that she was a sad, confused, unhappy, selfish, and unfortunately largely delusional writer whose talent never expanded to fill the enormous requirements of her output. But, still, the loss! *The loss!* The poetry of loss! What did Fitzgerald say so remarkably at the end of *Gatsby*? 'Borne back into the past, we beat off ceaselessly, banging like boats.' *Don't* quote me, Sweet Pea."

Curtis put down her pen.

"And, my dear, *blow* your nose, will you? The Kleenex is on the table. Your sniffing is driving me crazy. So, Georges, the CD player isn't working correctly, and the television, I don't know, the image is too wide."

"Too wide?"

He switched on the set.

"Yes, everything is a rectangle. It looks strange to me."

"It's a plasma television, Madame Steel; that is the shape of the screen."

"Well, I don't like it. I want it adjusted to look like a regular screen."

"I'll call electrics, but I'm not sure—"

"I'm sure for 3,300 euros a night you can make some sort of adjustment."

A soft knocking came at the door, and simultaneously the phone rang.

The door pushed open, and a middle-aged man rolled in a silver ice bucket containing a wine bottle. He had wispy gray hair, a round high forehead, and a broad prizefighter's nose. Curtis did a double take. He looked like someone she'd seen before; someone from the newspapers; someone involved in a scandal…. The man seemed a little startled that the room was filled with people. *"Excusez-moi,"* he whispered as he scrutinized the circle of occupants: Danielle Steel in bed, Curtis in the armchair, Georges attempting to adjust the size of the television image, the manager wheeling out the tableful of sad-looking fruit; Marcel and Cécélie sitting by the unlit fireplace. (They were Ms. Steel's massage therapist and nurse, shipped over from San Francisco.) Emerging from the bathroom, giggling, were two 23-year-old twins, Erin and Dana, also imported from San Francisco. They wore identical thick black eyeglasses, identical sneakers, identical lime-green tank tops, and identical James Baldwin tattoos on their inner forearms. They were staying down the hall in 220, and God only knew what their relationship was, these surreal, androgynous brunettes with the matching silver Tiffany necklaces that Steel had bought for them. She called them her "typists" and "editors." Most people in the Steel entourage were convinced the twins were actually writing the books. Apparently they were also "Barbara Cartland," "Mary Higgins Clark," and "Tony Kushner."

"What the hell is that?" asked Danielle in reference to the ice bucket. The phone was still ringing.

"With the compliments of the management," said the wine steward. He handed her a tiny cream-colored gift card.

"*Depuis combien de temps travaillez-vous ici?*" asked Georges.

"*Juste une semaine,*" said the wine steward, and he exited the room.

Danielle picked up the phone. "Yes, she is. Curtis, a Cyrano de Bergerac to see you? Are you kidding me? Sure you can send him up." She replaced the receiver. "Where the hell is my robe? Cécélie, get my robe. The blue room. The blue *robe*. Do you remember that, Georges?" She sang: "*We'll have a blue room/a new room/for two room…*You don't remember that? What the hell do you people know? Cécélie, the robe.

And who is Cyrano de Bergerac? Is this some boyfriend we don't know about, Sweet Pea?"

Curtis reddened a little. "No, it's the other interview I told you about."

"The interview?"

"The profile I'm doing for *Cahiers du Cinéma*. He's just calling himself Cyrano de Bergerac to elude the press."

"My God!" said Steel. "You mean it's Depardieu? Gérard Depardieu is coming up to my room, and I'm lying here in my Goddamn pajamas! Cécélie! My robe! My wig!" She ran into the bathroom. "My jewelry!"

"We're just walking over to Angelina's for lunch," said Curtis.

"One minute! One minute!" Steel stuck her head out of the bathroom. "Tell him I'll join you for a hot chocolate in an hour. Don't leave till I show up!"

"I don't know if the interview is going to *last* an hour."

"Charm him, Sweet Pea. And *blow* your nose."

Then the doorbell sounded.

Georges opened the door, and there entered the enormous figure of Gérard Depardieu. He was dressed in an open-collared white shirt and a summer suit of the palest green linen imaginable. In a sort of consciously casual juxtaposition to the perfectly tailored suit, he wore white sneakers.

The twins, Dana and Erin, let out a simultaneous gasp at his presence.

"Monsieur Depardieu?" asked Georges.

"As I've said to 10,000 women—*yes*," said Depardieu. He smiled winningly, and shook Georges's hand. "I have an appointment with—" he checked a memo pad—"Curtis Sittenfeld."

"That's me," said Curtis as she attempted to rise from her armchair. Her pink and green lanyard got stuck in the frame of the chair and nearly dragged her back into it. She was also painfully aware that "that's I" was the correct pronoun use.

"You'll have to excuse my surprise," said Depardieu. "I thought Curtis was a man's name."

"In America it usually is," she said, acutely aware that her sentence implied that in Europe it wasn't. She silently cursed her own stupidity once again.

He smiled and shook her hand.

Star voltage, the writer's voice in Curtis's head dictated to her. *His presence filled the room.* She became aware that there was a voice inside her who was writing the profile already, almost in spite of her, and she smiled, not so much at Depardieu but in grateful acknowledgement of that power within her. How long had she been aware of that gift? *Elementary school,* she thought, when even as a child (7? 8?) she'd been secretly convinced she was special and that her mission (her purpose?) was to walk through this planet with an invisible notepad in her hand, taking notes on herself. She was, in the words of Tom Stoppard, the "one lucky dog painting or writing about the other nine-hundred and ninety-nine."

Alpha-male, the voice inside her continued to dictate, and she longed to write in her journal but didn't want to appear overly self-conscious. You'd know in a second he was a celebrity. You could pick him out of a police line-up, having never seen him before, and know without a moment's hesitation that he was the film star. His radiant male presence of incandescent heterosexuality? Of certitude? Of easy confidence? Dressed in that effortless mantle of money and success which, curiously, made her acutely aware of her own femininity: an *unfolding* of her womanhood? She had felt, through most of the vast cloudy swath of her thirty years, like the girl at the party no one really wanted to sit with. Sure she had written *Prep* in her mid-twenties, a *New York Times* bestseller so successful that they sold the pink and green book strap of the front cover on her website! But still she felt, no, she *knew*, that her audience kept her at a distance. They had bought *Prep* by the thousands, all those lonely high school over-achievers who longed, in those pages, to find themselves, and so many of them were angry and disappointed when, somehow, they didn't. They had no shyness about telling her this at the signings and in their letters. *The book is well written but I hated Lee. She's such a whiney bitch…I just wanted to tell her to shut up, deal with it, and stop analyzing herself every time she wiped her ass.*

God, did any other major American novelist get letters like that? Curtis was the girl at the Advanced Placement lunch table who just sort of *smelled* funny, who tried too hard in her crooked teeth and her clunky shoes. The girl with the exposed midriff who was just a little too hefty to pull it off but felt she had to try anyway. Yet laugh as they might or hate her behind her back (*Curtis, we didn't know you wanted to go to the concert*) *she* was the one who had produced the novel; *she* was the one who had taken all the terror and misery of Cincinnati and all the casual psychological violence of the Groton School and fashioned it, within the crucible of her sad, little consciousness, into what she felt, no, she *knew* was an enduring work of American fiction. It was, as Wally Lamb had so perceptively written: "a voice as authentic as Salinger's Holden Caulfield and McCullers' Mick Kelly." She hadn't actually read Carson McCullers but she liked the comparison anyway. (She had tried to watch the film version of *The Member of the Wedding* one night on Turner Classic Movies but fell asleep.) She'd thought such a powerful endorsement from Wally Lamb would virtually guarantee her a spot on Oprah's book club, but, alas, that honor eluded her. She was hoping her new book, *The Man of My Dreams*, would finally open that magic Oprah door. She'd sit there in the Chicago studio, and Oprah would laugh her benevolently forgiving laugh, and the audience would line up at the microphone to ask Curtis questions: "Curtis, I never identified more in my *life* than I did with Hannah Gravener. She was me. (*Tearing up*) Curtis, I loved that book."

"Are you ready to go?" asked Depardieu.

"Of course," said Curtis who was fumbling to free her pink and green lanyard which had now gotten stuck in the fabric of the bedspread. Of course, *Curtis, I loved that book* was the response she had secretly hoped to get from male readers—or at least *one* male reader: one totally-irrational-I'm-enclosing-a-naked-photograph-of-myself male reader. The new book, she was convinced, would do this. And she didn't necessarily want to *marry* some male literary type who looked, in her mind, like a slightly unshaven Matthew McConaughey type—some open-shirted, Stetson-wearing, melancholy poet-sex-machine—well, okay, it wouldn't be *that* painful to marry a guy like that. But she wanted more to be finally in the presence of someone who just passionately *wanted* her; someone whose heart leaped up when she walked through the door. Instead of: *She looks better on the book jacket.* She looks a little, what? *Horsey?*

"We're off to Angelina's, correct?" asked Depardieu.

"One moment!" came Steel's strident voice from the bathroom. The door flew open, and she stood there, arms out theatrically. She was wearing a burgundy-colored bathrobe, and she'd affixed her perfectly coiffed wig and her large gold hoop earrings. Her lipstick was perfect, and she wore a copper-colored bracelet and a large copper-colored necklace whose links looked like a chain-link fence. "I'm a wreck! A total wreck! A mercilessly debauched and decrepit scribe! Ravaged by time!"

"Never, madame, never!" cried out Depardieu.

"God love you for the gorgeous French liar you are! Allow me to present myself. *Je m'appelle* Danielle Steel."

"The Danielle Steel who sells all those books?" asked Depardieu.

"Five hundred and fifty million but who *really* is counting?"

"Five hundred and fifty million and one. I just bought *Coming Out.*"

She held her hand to her heart. "I'm flattered, Monsieur Depardieu."

"Call me Géri."

"Then you must call me Danni."

"I began the novel last night. It is your greatest work yet."

"My greatest work is always the work yet to come," said Steel moving into the room. "But I must admit that Olympia Crawford Rubenstein may be my most engaging heroine to date. And that's a good lesson for you, *ma petite* Curtis. If they don't *love* your heroine, well, really, what *have* you got? And the heroine of *Prep*—and I'm not saying the book isn't *beautifully* written, my dear. God, I'd kill to have been your age and have written a sentence like: *He said, 'That was a great blow job,' and I felt prouder than if I'd gotten an A on a math test.* Magnificent! But, my dear, that girl of yours, what was her name? Jacqueline?"

"Lee."

"Yes, well, a *marvelous* character, but she's just so, I don't know what the word is in English...*overweight*—yes that's it, she's just so overweight that it's difficult to—and I don't mean *literally* overweight, no, God, dear me, I don't. I mean it metaphorically. She's just sort of *heavy* and *plodding*, you know? Four hundred and three pages of this increasingly *repellent* narrator? It gets *very* tiresome, my dear. As *mon petit* Géri knows, if the punters don't want to sleep with the leading man, they'll never come to see the show. Of course, in Géri's case, *every* woman in the audience wants to sleep with him."

"And most of them, unfortunately, have," said Depardieu.

"Yes," said Steel in the manner of a coming-attractions film narrator: "He was the man everyone wanted."

"And everyone got," added Depardieu with his lecherous leprechaun's smile.

"The film rights to *Prep* have been optioned to Paramount," said Sittenfeld a little stiffly.

"*Optioned*, well, we all know what *that* means," said Steel. "Money for nothing."

"And your chicks for free," said Depardieu.

They both laughed.

"Look at that face!" said Steel. She squeezed his cheeks. "Every woman in the world is in love with that face. Can you blame them?"

In Danielle Steel's head, time seemed to stand still, and in a near blinding moment of creative clarity she saw her next book standing in front of her—saw it as they say Mozart heard his music: complete in its entirety before a single note had been written. She even had the title: *Forever Loved, Forever Thin.*

She hurriedly sent them off to Angelina's; she would join them in an hour for a *chocolat africain*, but in the meantime there was a creative fever raging in her skull. She dismissed everyone except the twins, Erin and Dana, who sat giggling on the loveseat. She pulled off her wig and threw it at them.

Steel still wrote on a manual typewriter. She liked the Gutenbergian clack and heft of the metal type as it ratcheted under the fire of her imagination. Her old Olivetti stood on what looked like a hospital cart next to her bed; she swung it over, loaded in a piece of old-fashioned beige-colored newsroom copy paper, and began madly clacking away.

Forever Loved, Forever Thin. By Danielle Steel.

To Géri.

"And who could dream that love could come six times in one lifetime?"— d.s.

Outline.

HE: Stylish movie matinee idol. Is reported to have had 7,000 lovers BUT HAS NEVER HAD TRUE LOVE!!! French/American. Ripley deRochefort? Radziwill? Friends call him Rick. Owns club. Rick's Café Parisien. His face looks…

She stared at the place where Depardieu had stood, and the perfect word beautifully, miraculously came to her lips.

…chiseled.

His muscles something through his Armani suit—

She closed her eyes and visualized him again—

—rippled through his Armani suit.

She offered up a silent prayer to the muse of inspiration.

SHE: Semi-retired bestselling novelist. Finds love in books BUT NEVER IN REAL LIFE! Has been married ~~5~~ 2 times. Current bf is international publisher, ruthless Rupert

Murdoch type. Decent man but no sex and slightly overweight.
OTHER GIRL: Young assistant. Talented but tedious. Is writing a profile on Rick.
Her current bf is dull as shit herbal tea type.
Both women fall passionately for Rick despite his reputation. He's the criminal they ALWAYS fall for. The outlaw. The passion they NEED.
STORY: Love triangle! Will he choose youth or experience? Experience also=$!
Both women in ruthless cat fight to get him. Each has to juggle current bf!

First we think ~~Depardieu~~ Rick is playing with both of them. (Sex much better with older woman!) But, gradually, 300 pages?, we see him ACTUALLY FALL IN LOVE. He's falling in love with BOTH OF THEM. Hard. He's never felt anything like this before.

She ripped the paper from the typewriter and handed it to Erin and Dana as she headed for the shower. "Work with me," she said. "You'll need to add a pregnancy scare and a courtroom scene, and I think we've got the next book."

The taps were turned on in the bathroom.

"Awesome," said Erin, skimming through the outline.

"But what happens?" asked Dana. "Whom does he end up with at the end?"

Danielle stuck her head through the door. Steam poured around her.

"We won't know that for 24 hours, my dear." She laughed wickedly. "God, my life is like a Danielle Steel novel!"

***

Curtis Sittenfeld walked arm in arm with Gérard Depardieu down the second-floor staircase with its red, black, and gold Moroccan rug. They passed the enormous tapestry of pastoral figures playing flutes, and followed the wrought-iron handrail down to the marbled foyer. Carved on the wall was *César Ritz 1850-1918* and above it hung a modest brass portrait. The clock over the portrait—gold, roman-numeraled, looking like a larger-than-life pocket watch—indicated it was noon. Depardieu shook hands with a few fans. (It *was* true that everyone on earth recognized him.) Curtis picked up an *International Herald Tribune* from the front desk. She waited while Depardieu signed some autographs. He was laughing, speaking half-French, half-English. There was something slightly crouched in his gait, like a professional athlete ready to play. Her eyes took in the splendid blue carpet that extended from the front door to the entrance of the dining room, the marble columns: mottled pink and café au lait. The pattern of the marble looked like sea foam—or maybe the color and pattern of uncooked beef, threaded with yellow fat and clotted veins.

He took her arm once again, with a firmer grip than she would have expected, and they passed through the revolving door, descended the three red-carpeted steps, and walked out through the opened wrought-iron door under the round white awning that read Ritz Paris in pale blue script.

Tourists were taking pictures, and Curtis could hear the name *Depardieu* picked up softly by the crowd.

She became acutely aware of the word *celebrity*, and for a few indulgent seconds allowed herself to imagine that *she* was the famous one. *Celebrated American novelist Curtis Sittenfeld seen arm in arm with aging film star.* God help her, she *had* been celebrated in America, at least briefly, and she intuitively knew that with the publication of *The Man of My Dreams* she really *would* enter the ranks of the writers who genuinely mattered. Actually, she was there already. What had Alice Munro written in her blurb? "You feel there's a writer here who isn't trying to beguile you…. This is a courageous, refreshing novel." Daniel Menaker had called in quite a favor to get that quotation from Munro; she rarely blurbed fiction. *And yet,* thought Sittenfeld as she and Depardieu moved along the Place Vendome, there was something a little *less* than expansive in the quotation. A writer who isn't trying to beguile you? What on earth did that mean except here was a writer whom you didn't really *like.* Here was a narrator, who, once again, was a little repellent—a little heavy, plodding, trying too hard. It felt like a guarded, even *backhanded* compliment. And the second half? A courageous, refreshing novel? There was that terrible *hedge* again. Courageous was code for: she's willing to be *unlikable.* (The strange thing was that Curtis thoroughly believed Hannah Gravener was *infinitely* likable; readers would be falling in love with her.) And *refreshing*? Talk about a comment you didn't want to hear about a serious work of fiction. A refreshing novel? What the hell did that mean? *Refreshing* was a word you used for Diet Sprite. She had wanted Munro to have said: I loved this novel. I wanted to call up Curtis Sittenfeld the second I finished. I wanted to say, "Darling, I *loved* your book."

Depardieu was talking about a film he was preparing to shoot, and Sittenfeld knew she was supposed to be listening for her interview, but she was so overwhelmed by the sensory experience of Paris that it was difficult to stay focused. She thought it was the repellent ("courageous") part of her brain that finally forced her to say: "Look at the roofs all around the Place." She pointed towards the war memorial in the center of the octagon that formed the Place. "They call them Mansard roofs because they were invented by Jules Hardovin-Mansart. Mansart with a T."

Depardieu looked at the war monument. "As a child we used to sing about the monument." He suddenly sang in a beautifully musical, nearly operatic voice: *"Ah! qu'on est fier d'être français quand on regarde la Colonne!* That's what we call the monument. *La Colonne."*

"Wonderful."

"O monument vengeur, trophée indélébile."

"Indélébile is a beautiful word."

"It's only beautiful when *you* say it." He squeezed her arm affectionately.

Indelible would have been the perfect word for the blurb, she thought. Sittenfeld's Hannah Gravener has a voice so completely unique and so completely indelible that one savors it long after finishing the novel.

Why did they never write *that* one?

"Look," said Curtis. She was pointing again across the square. "You see where they're repairing the building?" A four-storey-high canvas curtain was suspended in front of ten arched doorways and their parallel windows. "They've actually *drawn* an outline of those doors and windows on the canvas, and it's perfectly lined up. Look, it's in perfect register with the real doorways and windows on the other side. Only in Paris would they do that. Make a piece of canvas beautiful just for the sake of beauty."

"How observant you are."

"In America they'd sell the space to advertisers. They'd paint an enormous Geico lizard up there."

"What color are your eyes?" asked Depardieu.

They turned left onto the Rue de Castiglione, and then another left onto the Rue de Rivoli. With its long line of antique, sand-colored, balconied apartments above the shops, the street felt to Curtis to be the perfect setting for her life. Across the street some pigeons rose from the black iron fence that outlined the park. Beyond the tall lamps that must have once been gas fixtures, she saw the trees.

She liked to rise early, hours before Danielle did, and sit in the Tuileries, under the shade of those trees, comfortably alone on the left side of a pair of upright metal chairs. She'd read the *Guardian* she'd bought at the English bookshop. She kept the receipts in her purse: *W.H. Smith France S.A.S., 248 Rue de Rivoli, 75001 Paris, Tel: 01 44 77 88 99*:

Pariscope (news)	*.40*
Guardian (news)	*3.00*
Total TTC TVA 0%	*3.40*
Especes	*10.00*
Rendu	*6.60*

Merci de votre visite et à bientôt

Every receipt had its own music, she thought, its own secret language. She'd saved the receipt from Walgreen's in Philadelphia before she left for this trip:

F TRJUN CNDM 3S	*5.99*
F TRJUN CNDM 3s	*5.99*
CMPBK 100SH	*.79 SALE*
CMPBK 100SH	*.79 SALE*
CMPBK 100SH	*.79 SALE*

Two packs of condoms and three school composition books! If the plane went down, her parents and friends could get a good laugh speculating about the receipt. "That was C. all right," her sister would say. "Always looking for possibilities." In truth, the purchase of the condoms was a little silly, but she didn't know the word in French and didn't want to embarrass herself in some little Parisian pharmacy with that green neon cross blinking outside.

The terrible truth—and she was ashamed to admit this even to herself—was that she had never actually experienced vaginal sex with a man. She had pleasured some guys—a handful of guys, wink, wink. (*Pleasured* was a tawdry word, she thought: smelling of Borax and wet sheets.) She'd been pleasured *by* some guys, but that raw ripe moment of watching some poor overwrought, unshaved slacker actually ejaculating (another horrible word) inside her had not yet occurred. That redolent reality had eluded her. By choice. And she was suddenly aware, walking down the Rue de Rivoli heading toward Angelina's, that the *terror* of being pregnant had loomed larger than any other force in her life. It was the terror of being *stuck*, the terror of sacrificing her career, her promise—because of some three-second transaction with some guy she probably didn't even like—*that* was unendurable.

She had written *Prep* about a not-so-ambitious girl face to face with the cruel strata of "social class in America" (Jennifer Egan, author of *Look at Me*); she had written *The Man of My Dreams* about a not-so-ambitious girl drifting through college and her first job at a counseling center in Albuquerque, but Curtis had yet to really explore the ghost who was operating the machine: the girl whose most urgent drive since junior high school was to *get published*. The girl who had mailed out twelve manuscript envelopes a week. The girl who wrote thank you letters to the editors who rejected her. ("I greatly appreciated the detail of your response....") The girl who battered *Seventeen* with her stories when she was fifteen! The girl whose life was a walking essay for *Salon* or maybe This American Life? Recipient of the Michener-Copernicus Society of America Award.

Now *that* was a character worth exploring. That was the next book.

"...the problem," continued Depardieu, "with reading glasses, when you're a middle-aged man like myself, is that you use the toilet to urinate, you look down to make sure everything's done, and then your glasses fall into the toilet!" He fingered his Clark-Kent-looking reading glasses. "You don't want to know where these have been!"

Rue de Rivoli, she thought, would be the name of the novel—a novella really, and the entire 100 pages of the story would be this one girl's thoughts. She's in her late 20s—and she walks along the Rue de Rivoli from Castiglione toward the Louvre. It would be a Virginia Woolf kind of story. We dip in and out of her thoughts as she passes each little tourist shop and corner café. *In one short walk of maybe twenty minutes, Sittenfeld manages, in a way that almost defies analysis, to encapsulate what it feels like to be young and alive at the beginning of the 21st Century. (Starred)*

"The idea of working with both Soderbergh and Scarlett Johansson—we're here—the dream of any actor working today."

The door to Angelina's was propped open to the clean August air. The pastries, dripping with raspberries, filled the front cases. The entire restaurant, in one half-second, had turned to observe the entrance of Gérard Depardieu, who didn't seem to notice.

"Somewhere in the back I think," he said. "And we're going to be joined by Madame Danielle Steel."

"With pleasure."

"I'm so glad to be here with you," said Depardieu, moving towards their table. "I'm just in awe of your work."

"You've read my novel?"

"One moment, *chérie*," he said, and indicated by his hands that he desired to wash up.

The restrooms in Angelina's were upstairs and, as Depardieu disappeared up the curved stairs, Curtis sat a small table and looked for the first time at her copy of the *International Herald Tribune*. The newspaper reprinted articles from *The New York Times*, and, that particular morning, Sittenfeld was shocked to see, on the arts page, a tiny photograph of herself. It took the wind right out of her. She actually looked around the restaurant to see if anyone else was reading the paper. Next to her photograph read the headline: *The Myopic Navel Gazer Can't See Her Way to Love* by Janet Maslin.

Curtis swallowed hard. She felt sick.

Her eyes moved down the column:

...her first novel, the defiantly ordinary "Prep."

...Miss Sittenfeld's embrace of the unremarkable is even clingier the second time around.

Angelina's suddenly felt airless, and the glow that had illuminated her entrance with Depardieu extinguished. Someone put a menu in front of her. *"Merci,"* she said automatically, but her eyes continued down the column:

...her drab heroine is made special mainly by endless reserves of myopia and self-pity.

...a flat, present-tense style meant to replicate intimacy.

There were actually tears rising in her eyes. She looked again around the restaurant. Depardieu was descending the stairs. Patrons lounged around her sipping hot chocolate and eating toast points, and here she sat, drowning inside her worst nightmare: public humiliation.

Maslin quoted one sentence after another, each, out of context, sounding progressively more ludicrous.

"Hannah becomes conscious of how foamy her pillow feels…"

"This is why Hannah fell for Oliver: because he took out her splinter."

The book offers no evidence to the contrary. Its world is really that small.

"Anything good in the paper," asked Depardieu heartily. "I'm starving! Have you ordered?"

She couldn't even see him anymore, and she became conscious that her appetite, like her blood, seemed literally to have drained out onto the floor.

She folded the newspaper and placed it under her chair.

A commotion at the door. Entering at top-volume were Danielle Steel and her entourage: Dana and Erin, her massage therapist, her nurse.

"Oh, dear," said Curtis as her eyes moved to the Ugly American and Her Posse. "We're going to need a bigger table."

"Look," said Depardieu, and here, sickeningly, he reached under the table for her newspaper. "We're never going to get a moment's privacy, and I've got a proposition for you."

"A proposition?"

He took out his Waterman pen and wrote on the corner of the newspaper: *Le Dauphin, Rue St. Honoré/Place André Malraux.* "Let's have dinner tonight at, say, 10? Is that too late?"

"No, no."

"Go to this restaurant." He pointed to the newspaper.

"Tell them you're with me. Okay?" He was holding her hand. "It's going to be very special."

"Very special."

He laughed and pointed a short meaty finger at the newspaper picture. "She looks a little like you!"

Danielle's voice rang across the restaurant. "Thank *God* we're not too late! Charles, *chocolat africain* for everyone at my table. Seven!"

"I don't like hot chocolate," said Curtis.

"Work with me, Sweet Pea."

Curtis felt as if she were falling backwards. Vomit rose in her mouth, and she forced it back down. It wasn't even the negative tone of the review that bothered her so much as it was the outrageous inaccuracy of its observations. Myopic navel gazing?! So any serious work of fiction that purported to examine a character's inner life was myopic navel gazing?

Curtis rose. "Excuse me, I'm suddenly very warm. I need to wash up."

Danielle had already begun her loud critique of the menu. "They used to have the sole. I love the sole. Why on earth they got rid of the Goddamn sole I'll never know."

Depardieu turned to Curtis. "Are you all right, my dear?" He seemed genuinely concerned.

"She's fine," said Steel.

Curtis practically ran up the stairs, but her green and pink lanyard got caught in the railing and practically yanked her down again.

She bolted the bathroom door. There were cloth towels with *Angelina's* stitched in their center in gold script. She wet a towel and wiped her face and neck. When her gaze rose to the mirror she was astonished to see she still looked healthy and balanced and sane. The old Curtis. The same face she'd had at seventeen. She let the muscles in her cheeks unclench, and it seemed to her that, at rest, her face had something forgiving in it. *"The quality of mercy is not strained,"* she quoted to her reflection.

Checking that the door was bolted, she cleaned her glasses to examine herself more closely. "You'll survive this," she said aloud. Then she completely unbuttoned her blouse and used the moistened washcloth to cool down her shoulders and neck and breasts and stomach. She found that looking at herself half-dressed in the mirror was a mildly erotic experience. For this reason she usually got dressed very quickly after a shower. But this time she permitted her gaze to linger at the shadowy even curvaceous figure before her. The light through the side window, reflecting against the white tile walls, was soft and particularly flattering. Even her stomach looked kind of pretty, and as she looked at her navel she thought it was the one orifice of the body that wasn't charged with sexual potency. The mouth was alluring. The ears with their tiny flower-bud intricacy were adorned with sparkly silver to make the male butterfly look twice. But the poor navel—as sensually neutral as a big toe or a finger-print—just a pointless flourish of profligate nature.

A knocking at the door broke her reverie.

"Are you done in there?"

Sittenfeld, a little guiltily, buttoned her shirt.

A messenger from the Ritz appeared in the door of Angelina's clutching a large manuscript envelope which was elaborately stamped with overnight delivery stickers. The messenger huddled in animated conference with the maître d', and then threaded his way towards Steel.

"Madame, pardon, you must sign for these."

"My proofs!" squawked Steel so loudly that strangers turned to look. In truth, she knew they were looking already: her "rusty" Guccissima soft leather handbag, her Chintamani diamond hoop earrings looking like ornate treble clefs, her matching Chintamani diamond ring looking like three pairs of opera glasses fused together—so large she couldn't actually bend the knuckle of her right ring finger. Her dress was a simple, elegant sleeveless Dolce & Gabbana silk cherry-print with black spaghetti straps and black ribbed lace around the décolletage. Its splash of color was set off beautifully, she felt, by her white calfskin Coco boots with their patent leather toes. Though they looked marvelous, even the short walk from the Ritz had caused her severe tendon pain and nearly a traffic accident. Crossing Rue d' Alger, the heel of her right boot had stuck in the storm grate. "Evan!" she'd shrieked. She was suddenly lopsided and stalled on the side of the street. Her massage therapist strode out of the crowd and lifted her up and out.

"Who's got a pen? Quick, I need a pen! Come on! Where's my writer's bag! I need my bag!"

The twins, Dana and Erin, had produced a serious-looking Chanel alligator doctor bag.

"You're going to correct proofs right at the table?" asked Curtis

"They're holding up production till I sign off on these."

Danielle tore open the FedEx envelope and carefully extracted the contents. She produced a neat stack of about sixty 11x14 color photographs of herself. "For my readers," she explained to Depardieu, "the jacket photograph is *critical*. Now, Géri, you *have* to help me. We need one for the jacket and an entirely *different* one for the four-color, double-page display ad." She turned to Dana and Erin. "Get me a pen! I need to do the color corrections."

The twins were furiously digging through her writer's bag. Out came the mirrors, the make-up tubes, lipsticks, rejuvenating creams.

"Oh, for God's sake, I'll do it with lip liner," she said as she blanched with horror at the first photograph. *"Oh-my-God!"* She smeared the dark brown lip liner in a messy X across a nearly monochromatic photograph of her dressed as a sort of Carnaby Street jockey: a huge white double-breasted Nicholas Ghesquiere wool coat that made her look like David Byrne in *Stop Making Sense.* The massive white tent was accented by black leather gloves, knee-high black leather boots, and a black Oliver Hardy hat that was taller than the length of her entire face.

She flipped to the next one, and she literally *screamed.*

A waiter dropped a pile of plates in reaction.

"Nanook of Newark!" she cried. "It would be funny if it wasn't so hopelessly horrible." The photo showed her, in a massive brown wig of curls, enveloped in a Prada black leopard coat with a fox-fur bodice, black leopard velvet pants, black cashmere leg warmers, and a Marc Jacobs beret that looked like a gigantic hairnet. To add to this wintry intensity, she was wearing jet-black lipstick and black nail polish. "I look like the Slut of Siberia."

"None of these even marginally captures your charm," said Depardieu.

"Did you hear that?" Steel said to Dana and Erin. "Did you hear what the man said? *Change my will.* Immediately. Géri gets the Patek Philippe."

"Merci."

"26,300 euros. But who's counting? Hmmm..." She

scrutinized the next one. "Who's got glasses? Quick!" While the twins were fumbling through the writer's bag, Depardieu offered her his reading glasses. "Thanks so much." She sniffed the frames. "I love your cologne. What do you think of this? Does it work for the jacket?"

The photo showed her, with windblown brown hair cascading down to her forearms, dressed in nothing but a light pink bra with lace trim and hipster panties.

A long pause, and finally Sittenfeld said: "Courageous."

"*Courageous?* What the hell do you mean by that?"

"Just…you know…courageous and refreshing?"

"What are you saying? That a woman *of a certain age* can't dress like this?"

"No, I—"

"Do you have any idea how many *hundreds* of thousands of dollars are reflected in this picture? I could have built you a house, Sweet Pea, on what you're looking at in Thermage, Botox, and Restylane—not to mention the vaginoplasty—so do me a favor and wipe the little shocked smirk off your face."

"I think what she means," said Depardieu, "is whether it's right for a book jacket."

"I'm afraid I have to go to the bathroom again," said Sittenfeld, and she fled the table.

"Hmmm," said Steel, still scrutinizing every inch of the photograph. "Maybe you're right. Maybe we'll save it for the *Book Review* ad.*"

"You look lovely," said Depardieu. "But then I've never seen you when you haven't looked lovely."

"Girls, we're using that line on the jacket."

"May I have my glasses back?"

He touched her hand.

She suggestively toycd with the frames of his glasses in her mouth. "You'll come by my room for dinner tonight?"

He nodded.

"It will have to be early," he said. "We're working early tomorrow. Six?"

She lowered her voice. "We might be working late tonight. Ten."

"Eight?"

"Nine," she said as if this were the sexiest word ever spoken in Paris.

Curtis Sittenfeld, dressed in what she hoped was at least a semi-alluring white cardigan over a pale blue button-down shirt, sat by herself in a Häagen-Dazs on the Left Bank. She was too nervous to eat any real dinner, and, anyway, she imagined, her real dinner would be at 10 p.m. at Le Dauphin. She'd walked by a few times earlier that evening on the pretext of checking out the menu. It was a narrow intimate-looking place on the right side of Rue Saint Honoré. Closed in the early evening, the window was full of awards and recommendations. That she had already decided on the house specialty, prime-rib (serves two), struck her as one of her more disagreeable traits: her need, always, to over-plan, to work through all the possibilities ahead of time.

It was exhausting and dispiriting.

She'd ordered two scoops of chocolate chocolate-chip, and now that the waxed cup was put in front of her, it looked too large, too sweet, too excessive—even slightly sickening. Still, she ate it. What the hell. August in Paris. *Whom can I run to?* She stared at the receipt.

Häagen-Dazs
96 BD ST GERMAIN
75005
1 COMPO 2 BOULES 5.00

And still she half-hoped for the tap on the shoulder.

"Excuse me, are you American? I saw you sitting here alone, and I thought, well, if you didn't mind, that maybe I could join you?"

As she left, a handsome young Frenchman in a military green short-sleeved shirt followed her out. "Excuse me?" he said.

She turned.

He wore the ghost of a moustache.

"I think you dropped this."

He handed her the *Eyewitness Guide to Paris* that had fallen from her bag.

"Thank you so much."

He smiled, then he returned inside. She imagined that he would never think of her again for the rest of his life.

She, however, knew she would think of him often. Perhaps he would even appear in one tiny scene in her next novel.

Across the street, over by the statue of Danton pointing dramatically to his right, some kind of protest was going on. She heard voices amplified by a megaphone; she saw a red cloth banner with black iron-on letters spelling out a quotation from Victor Hugo. Without putting on her glasses, she strained to make out the words:

...*Je me sens la frén*...(letters wrapped around the tree)...*de tous les hommes et l'hâte de tous les peuples.*

She bought an hour of Internet time at a humid little arcade:

XS Arena St. Michel
Username: jfvuik
Password: uggnvt
Temps: 1h
Caissier: DouDou

She imagined that the sympathy notes for her terrible review in the *Times* might be posted by now. The condolence letters from her friends and editors...even her mother and sister would have weighed in by now.

Nothing. There were seven messages. They were all advertising. Her Poland Spring water delivery was scheduled for tomorrow.

Not a word.

Were they hoping that she just hadn't seen it?

Why spoil her trip to Paris?

With one review, she thought, Curtis Sittenfeld had become box office poison. Anyone even remotely associated with her picked up her stink of failure.

Keep away. She's a hopeless lightweight. She's yesterday's *wunderkind.*

She found a movie memorabilia store, Ciné Reflet, on the Rue Serpente, and she thought she might buy something special for Depardieu. The store smelled wonderfully of old posters and yellowing magazines. She wished, briefly, that she had come to Paris with a friend who could photograph her browsing in this magical store. It would make an awesome author photo.

She bought a 1984 vintage issue of *Cahiers du Cinéma* for 18 euros. It was a tribute issue celebrating the life of François Truffaut. She was pleased with the purchase (and, okay, she had also bought a postcard of Depardieu as Cyrano. They could have fun with that later: "I hear a man's nose is related to the size of his ego," she'd say coyly.) But how on earth could Maslin accuse her of navel gazing? God, that stuck in her craw! She was buying a vintage magazine that *he* would love; it had nothing to do with her. It took every ounce of moral strength to keep her from shooting off an e-mail to *jmaslin@nytimes.org*. She wanted to protest the *inaccuracy* of the review. She could defend every sentence that Maslin quoted. "He had removed her splinter" wasn't just about removing a *splinter* for God's sake. It was about how a small moment could, with enough reflection, grow into a potent symbol.

"Have you been to Truffaut's grave?" asked the clerk in a beautifully accented English; he'd realized she was an American. He was in his thirties. Extremely close-cropped hair. She thought he looked more like a professional runner than a guy who worked in a cinema bookstore. "The Cimetière de Montmartre. On the hill. Very beautiful."

"Really?"

"A perfectly flat black marble slab. No headstone of any kind. Surrounded by ancient and elaborate graves. Heine. Berlioz. And then there is this stone. Almost blank. Then one sees the small engraved letters. *François Truffaut. 1932-1984.* That's it. Nothing more. Always flowers on it. Anytime you go, always fresh flowers."

"Lovely."

"You admire Truffaut." He indicated her copy of *Cahiers du Cinéma.*

"A friend does."

"Fifty-two years old. Terrible. Terrible."

"What did he die of?"

"No one is quite sure. Godard said he was tired of

living. Can such a thing be? Did you ever see Truffaut's *The Green Room*?"

She shook her head no.

"It is a man saying goodbye to life."

Standing in the store, staring into the eyes of this poet-clerk, she suddenly felt she was a moment away from crying.

Back in Room 201 at the Ritz, sixty-seven votive candles were burning. The air smelled of vanilla and Vitabath. Across this heady cathedral of luminescence stood Danielle Steel and Gérard Depardieu. *Time stood still,* thought Steel whose brain, in her last fleeting seconds of rationality, was transfiguring this tableau into art.

Depardieu took a quick glance at his watch. Then he moved a step closer.

Steel stood stock-still: an animal on the alert to either kill or be killed. She didn't care particularly which one it was. The scent of musk rose around her like the mist of her own desire. The Chanel volumizer had expanded her hair into the storm-tossed mane of a temptress. Her Alexander McQueen outfit consisted of a rope-colored cowl-neck sweater whose cowl was so huge it fell down her neck to her midriff. It hung around her neck like an inner tube, exposing a passionate ellipse of chest which shone conspicuously brassiereless underneath the capacious cowl. The sleeves of the sweater were so long that only her fingertips could be seen. A leather belt tethered her midriff about six inches above the bottom of the sweater which fell over a tiger skin knee-length dress and Vuitton heels that perfectly matched her rope-colored sweater. The tiger skin felt perfect. It felt like her own skin, like the flag of her own primitive carnality. What was the Ritz anyway but a kind of rough-hewn clearing in the forest, a tiny man-made platform two stories up from the savagery of the streets? They might have been standing in the middle of the Amazon rainforest. He stood there, still in his lime-green Armani sports jacket, and he might have been the first man on earth. And she stood there. She was Everywoman, the first woman, the last woman, the eternal woman, and she knew, she *felt*, she was radiating lust and fear and the unquenchable thirst to fuse with the completely male entity who stood before her.

"Sorry I'm late," he said. "And I've got to be out by ten. I'm shooting with Soderbergh tomorrow."

He took another step forward.

She wanted to stop him. She wanted to stop him as he plunged his hot face into the bare flesh of her cowl-neck sweater. She wanted to tell him to wait. She wanted to say the words *slow down*. But the worst of it was that she didn't want him to wait. She didn't want him to slow down. He devoured her face in kisses, and she thought: This is the reason mankind built Paris: so one ferocious, ruthless man— his chiseled face, his taut muscles rippling through the fabric of his perfect Armani suit—could possess this one woman. Her womanhood expanded in his arms, unfolding, widening in wonder. It was nature. It was instinct. It was beyond her control. He picked her up in his arms and she felt oddly boneless. She could no longer resist.

She felt herself falling back onto the bed. She might have been falling onto the leaf-strewn forest floor in the Garden of Eden. He said nothing. He wanted her and she wanted him. It was as simple as that. She could no longer resist. The power of the universe had brought them together. He undressed her. She wanted to stop him. But she didn't want to stop him. Before she knew how it happened they were both naked and he was making love to her. And though their lives and backgrounds were worlds apart they both knew that they had found each other. It was a miracle that God had brought them together, and they clung to each other, drowning in their passion.

He looked down at her, his eyes filled with love. He said: "I think the condom might have ripped."

It was 10:20 and Curtis Sittenfeld stood outside Le Dauphin Restaurant in the rainy Parisian darkness waiting for her date. Two French girls in their early twenties pulled up in their Smart car and parked in an impressively small space. Before they emerged she could see the blue glow of the driver's cell phone. They got out: cigarettes and cell phones and slinky black dresses, and they headed across the Place André Malraux, their heels clicking. They stopped in the middle of the plaza, two silhouettes, and checked their text-messages once again. Sittenfeld thought: All over Paris tonight young men and women are arranging to make love. You felt it in the air; it was the second half of the double feature: first, the Ernst Lubitsch retrospective at Le Champo, then the main attraction: the peeling of the clothes, the startling visibility of the flesh. She laughed to herself at both the allure of it and the grotesque predictability of it. Everyone knew the end of the play.

She became aware of the feel of the pavement beneath her clunky chock-a-block shoes. The cold of the streets was seeping into her feet. Then she became conscious of the sounds around her: the wind whipping the awning of Le Dauphin, the sudden eruption of laughter from the bar inside. When the door opened she heard the soft sounds of the silverware and the wine glasses, the Billie Holiday CD playing inside: *Comes a mousey/You can chase it with a broom.* If she listened carefully enough she could even hear her own breathing; she imagined she could even hear her own heart. *Comes love/There ain't nothing you can do!*

"Curtis!" yelled a voice down the street.

From where she stood she could see, far down the left side of the Rue Saint Honoré, the figure of Gérard Depardieu.

He's running for me, she thought. And she suddenly recognized that, in some strange and certain and purely irrational way, she loved him.

How extraordinary!

"Thank God you're still here," she heard him saying. He was completely out of breath. "I was so scared you wouldn't wait."

He was like a little boy: voice breaking, hair mussed, shirt barely tucked in.

Curtis thought: I love him because he's my beautiful, sensitive boy.

Gérard Depardieu kept an apartment on the Rue Goethe, almost across the street from the Musée d'Art Moderne where Sittenfeld herself had stood in line to see the Bonnard exhibit. The Rue Goethe was a quiet, tree-lined street that reminded Curtis of the more elegant neighborhoods of Manhattan. She could imagine herself living on the Rue Goethe, walking past the performance arts center along the winding back alleys, with a bottle of Evian in her hand and all the time in the world.

This particular evening, however, she found herself tied to one of the posts of the antique cherry-wood bed that practically filled Depardieu's entire apartment. She was nude, her wrists were bound lightly with her pink and green lanyard, and she was lying face down on the sheetless bed. Depardieu had explained, with a childlike sense of apology, that all the sheets were out being washed.

A noisy ceiling fan turned in a slightly off-balance orbit. It reminded her of a record on a turntable that was slightly misaligned.

"You're going to enjoy this!" said Depardieu. He was still completely dressed, and she looked over her shoulder (*Decreased range of motion,* she thought. Surely a sign she was getting older.) to see him pivot off the bed and remove from the armoire some heavy-looking piece of machinery about the size of an electric broom. *"This* is going to make you feel like a woman," he said. "This is the secret every French woman knows."

She heard him strenuously yanking what sounded like the pull-cord to a gasoline-powered lawnmower. It took him three tries before the motor caught, and it sounded as loud as if there actually were a lawn mower in the room.

"Won't the neighbors complain?" she asked as loudly as she could.

"Are you kidding? I've got a waiting list to borrow this. Here, *ma chérie.*"

He gently clipped around her head a pair of noise-suppressing headphones.

"Much better, right?" she heard his muffled voice say,

Actually it was better, and she looked over her shoulder (*decreased range of motion*) with a slightly detached curiosity to see that affixed to the end of the machine, which was so heavy that he could barely support it with both hands, was a strawberry-colored rubber device, about the size of an industrial flashlight. It was spinning like a drill bit. He was moving it with delicious slowness towards her .

"Now, when your readers ask you to define what love is," he said, "you tell them this!"

"What exactly do I tell them?" she shouted.

"You tell them: 'Mr. Twisty.'"

She turned her head back towards the bedpost, and she thought about the line quoted in the Janet Maslin review: *Hannah becomes conscious of how foamy her pillow feels.* Actually, it really wasn't a bad line, especially when you balanced its syntactical rhythm with the second half of the sentence: "then she becomes conscious of how stuffy the room is." The word "stuffy" actually worked well, she felt, because it was so perfectly freighted with connotations about the suffocating smallness of Hannah's own life.

She heard Depardieu gun the speed control of the machine—like a dentist warming up his drill.

With her chin resting deep in the pillow, she became conscious of how foamy the pillow really *was.* She wondered, briefly if Target sold Tempur-Pedic pillows like this one. She'd buy two. One for herself and one for her mom.

The Ritz pool is located in the basement of the hotel. One descends through a series of circular staircases, past some administrative desks, and finally finds oneself moving through a sort of cement wading pond, past the Jacuzzis, into the pool room.

Danielle and Curtis had agreed to meet there before breakfast for a swim, and both seemed silent and reflective— as if the emotions of the previous night had so filled them to the brim that there was little room left for words.

Steel was thinking about wedding rings.

Sittenfeld was thinking about how to say, "I need to see a gynecologist" in French.

The pool, with its airy, elegant Greco-Roman pillars, was so well lit that it seemed to be outdoors. The marble walls were printed with two enormous frescos: elegant long-necked ladies in blue and hay-colored togas standing on balconies overlooking the cypress trees. Black lamps with white shades stuck out from each pillar like an arm. The towering ceiling picked up the Greco-Roman motif. Painted vines wound around the ceiling's wide expanse. The center was filled with the image of sun-lit clouds. At the circumference of the clouds a few figures in togas could be seen as if they were leaning over a stone border, looking down into the pool.

The room was completely empty except for Steel and Sittenfeld floating in the turquoise water. Somewhere off to the side, a white-haired pool attendant was shuffling about.

There was the loud click of what might have been a door locking. It was so unnaturally loud in the echoing room that Sittenfeld turned in alarm.

Nothing.

The water was deliciously warm.

Sittenfeld remembered Pamela Harriman had drowned in this pool some years earlier. She wondered if the guests now stayed away.

She could hear some piped-in classical music with the volume turned just a little too low.

"What a night," sighed Steel. She was floating on her back. She wore a white bathing cap and the pink bikini briefs she had worn in her book jacket photo-shoot. Sittenfeld wore a more modest orange one-piece. She was floating on her back as well, wondering if her date with Monsieur Twisty was going to render her childless for the rest of her life or maybe just force her to get a colonoscopy. Then she swam underwater and dreamed of finding a hidden portal there— an unexplored opening that would take her a million miles from the Danielle Steels of the world. And, really, how was she supposed to write a portrait of this woman for *Poets and Writers*? She'd been with her a week and, in truth, she'd barely listened to a word Steel had said. She was sick of Steel and of the *Times* and of books and of herself and this never-ending drain on her energy to be *noticed,* to be observant, to gather the pithy insights for her next essay. "Curtis, this is A.O. Scott from *The New York Times*...we're asking writers to name the three most influential books of fiction produced in the last 100 years, and we're hoping you'd like to participate. We're calling the article *In Search of the Best.*"

She had e-mailed him back:

Ulysses, James Joyce.

Prep, Curtis Sittenfeld.

The Man of My Dreams, Curtis Sittenfeld (forthcoming)

It was like voting for senior superlatives in high school. You just had to get the numbers up. But maybe Scott had called Maslin. Maybe her review was payback for Sittenfeld's arrogance. But it *wasn't* arrogance. She was being satirical. Well, semi-satirical. *Prep* was a pretty extraor-dinary book. Other than *To Kill a Mockingbird* she couldn't think of a better first novel. And everybody knew Capote wrote *Mockingbird*.

Steel, meanwhile, was feeling empty. She longed to feel luxuriant, to feel full of possibilities, but she felt only a sort of post-coital emptiness. Or maybe post-cowl-neck emptiness. Morning came. The sun rose...and what did she have to show for all that yearning? All that animalism? All that primitive coupling on the desert of loneliness? What did she have to show for it? A tigerskin dress torn in two? A ripped condom? When she tried to focus on the specific memory of his manhood, it looked less and less like a scepter of virility, and more and more like a half-cooked Hebrew National Bun-buster. *Oy.* How many more books was she going to write anyway? How many more interviews with lumpy little interns like this one? How many more earrings? How many more pairs of shoes? Maybe she could just float here forever, and, finally, in a few thousand years, her poor body would begin to unlock, would begin to stop caring so much, stop *needing* so much.

The white-haired pool attendant in his black service tuxedo pulled his rolling towel cart towards them. Stooped, ancient. *He's been here since Roman times,* thought Steel. Serving the rich and powerful for tips. It was sad really.

Steel and Sittenfeld both swam to the edge of the pool. Then they hoisted themselves heavily out of the water, and sat shivering on the pool's lipped edge.

The pool man turned slowly around to face them.

It was Sittenfeld who gasped first.

The pool man was smiling broadly.

It was Steve Martin.

He rolled his eyes and spoke with a swooping, Great Gildersleeve, comic-salesman's zaniness. "Can I *offer* you ladies anything! Perhaps something in a *towel*! *Yay*-ess!" Then he smiled like a demented Jack o' lantern and went cross-eyed. *"Her-her-her-HER-her!"*

FOUR

MEIN LIEBLING, MEIN ROSE

Even the *Bangor Daily News* (arguably the worst newspaper in America) ran the story on page one. It ran just under: *The American Folk Festival/Bangor/4 Days to Go!* and slightly to the right of: *"The tossing of a frozen pig's head into a Lewiston mosque last week has upset Muslims in Central Maine...."*

The story that caught Stephen King's eye that noisy morning—Chimichanga Lawn Concepts was outside riding back and forth on their huge mower—ran under the subhead: *Writers' Deaths Like Something from a Novel—Reuters.* The lead ran: *The nearly featureless skeletons of writers Danielle Steel and Curtis Sittenfeld ("Prep") were discovered late yesterday morning in the Jacuzzi of the Ritz Hotel in Paris. In a crime that might have come from the mind of Stephen King—*

"Thanks for the name-check," said King aloud. *The mind of Stephen King.* People threw that phrase around as if his mind were some kind of large tumor sitting crookedly on his shoulders. He had half-seriously suggested to TNT that the next series be called: *From the Ass of Stephen King.* He had even suggested the first story: *The Biggest Bowel Movement in Bangor.* He'd actually begun writing it: an alien spore causes a massive red tide in Maine, and the contamination avalanches into an epidemic of unstoppable shitting. All over the state: schools; industrial parks; 4H clubs; all anyone in the state is doing is shitting. The sewage treatment plants can't handle the deluge. It's like the Hurricane Katrina of Shit. Spike Lee films a documentary about it—*The Day the Whites-Only Toilets Broke: A Bowel In Four Movements.* Lines at portable toilets stretch seven blocks. A sign reads: *Warning: Do Not Defecate in Public Lakes and Streams. It's Not Only Illegal, It's a Health Hazard!* Of course, it was hard to read the sign because it was buried under a 20-foot pile of shit. The story was probably too grotesque for mainstream television, but he figured he could always sell it to Posthumous Press. Those guys would buy anything.

According to Paris police, the two writers were found chained to cinderblocks at the bottom of the Jacuzzi. A hydraulic pumping device was apparently used to fill the Jacuzzi with what police chemists now believe was glacial sulphuric acid.

When authorities at the Ritz finally opened the locked doors of the pool room, at approximately 2 p.m., concierge Georges Gharbi came upon a scene of horror that seemed scarcely believable. "The room smelled of chemicals. The water in the Jacuzzi was a yellowish brown. A mist hung in the air. In the Jacuzzi were two skeletons. Their ankles were still chained to cinderblocks."

The body of bestselling romance writer Danielle Steel, 60, was identified by staff at the hotel. The other body was identified as writer Curtis Sittenfeld, 30, who was staying at the hotel to profile Ms. Steel for Poets and Writers.

The corpse of Ms. Steel was found with its arms outstretched as if she was struggling to get to the surface. The body of Ms. Sittenfeld was found folded in on itself, skull stuck in the direction of its navel.

King felt his hands shaking as he flipped to page A28 for the details. The phone had been ringing all morning; he hadn't picked up. Journalists asking for a comment.

His right leg was shaking uncontrollably.

First Sue Grafton disappeared down Reichenbach Falls. Now, barely a week later, Steel and Sittenfeld murdered. Unless it was the most bizarre case of joint suicide the world had ever recorded. But he'd met Danielle Steel.

There was no way that ambitious broad was ever going to kill herself. Not as long as there was one more version of *Love's Pulsing Pudendum* to write.

Grafton gone, Steel gone, Sittenfeld gone…it sounded like the plot of some terrible literary parody.

King wandered into the kitchen and brewed himself another cup of licorice-tasting herbal tea that his acupuncturist had told him would cure his allergies. He drank it three times a day. It did nothing but give him a splitting headache. Poor Dr. Chang! She could barely understand English. "How you bladder?" she asked him the other day, and he was impressed, once again, by the mysteries of Eastern medicine—that she could look at his tongue and fingernails and ascertain, like some diminutive magician, his deep internal problems. "My bladder is fine," he said. "It's my neck and shoulder that are killing me." She nodded vigorously and continued to tap her tiny needles into his scalp and legs. Then, five minutes later: "You bladder? He writer like you?"

"My *brother*?"

"Yah, you bladder."

So much for the mysteries of Eastern medicine.

And now his blood work came back last week showing he was slightly low in phosphorus. 2.2 mg/dL. His ancient and powerful tome of research—*Reader's Digest's Healing Power of Vitamins, Minerals, and Herbs*—indicated that low phosphorus levels were rare. Possible indication of kidney or bowel trouble…. Christ, not only was he hit by a Dodge truck, he had cancer-coated kidneys. When he looked in the mirror now he saw the unshaved, underweight ghost of who he'd once been. It was genuinely frightening.

He'd heard an interview the other morning on the radio about a jazz record called *Walking with the Wazmo*—the wazmo, apparently, was hipster slang for confidence and swagger. He looked at the old book jacket photo of himself on the back of *Christine*, sitting on the hood of that Plymouth under a garage sign that read *Exit Only*—the legend below: *Stephen King and friend*. There he sat, fingers interlaced, shit-kicker boots, aviator glasses, all that dark hair—and the look in his dopey gap-toothed smirk said: Yo, man, I've got the wazmo. I've written another hit. Another movie. Another cover of *Newsweek* ("The Stephen King Phenomenon").

Christ, he once *was* a phenomenon. Now he was a skinny douche bag with low phosphorus and iron bars on his windows and the one girl he'd tricked into loving him had finally seen through his bullshit and left him for good. "Stephen, you're just too crazy to live with. You want to write, then you cut yourself completely off from the world. How fucked up is that? What are you going to write about?"

"Tabby, aren't you the one who gave me *Letters to a Young Poet*? Do you remember that? 'And even if you were in prison the walls of which let none of the sounds of the world come to your senses—would you not then still have your childhood, that precious kingly possession, that treasure house of memories?'"

"What are you talking about, Stephen?"

"I'm going *inside*, Tabby. I'm going Marlow."

And as he'd said the words, he'd thought: Jesus, I *am* going crazy.

How had she stayed with him 35 years? He thought of her now: her curls, the shape of her lips, the smell of her skin.

He wanted to fall to the ground and beg her forgiveness.

He was alone in this fucking prison of a house, and Mr. Top Ten with a Bullet had King's name on his list. King's name *had* to be on the list. All the bestselling authors—one after the other. Hey, he'd *fight* to be on the list, *pay* to be on the list. What kind of second-rate loser didn't make the list? Some mid-list wannabe like T. Coraghessan Boyle? Jesus, he ought to be killed just for the pretentiousness of his name. Okay, King's name was definitely on the list. *Top* of the list. But what was the motive? (Reginald Denny as Inspector Lestrade: "Moteeve? What moteeve? 'ho cares about moteeve?") Jealousy? Revenge? Some sort of Robert James Waller-type? Some guy who can't crack the bestseller list a second time? And it's driving him insane? That might be a place to start. Or maybe some fundamentalist psycho who saw popular literature as impure? Destroy the infidels! Kill Curtis Sittenfeld! Yeah, that made a lot of fucking sense. *Literary Jihadists Vow to Kill Michiko Kakutani Once They Figure Out How To Pronounce Her Name.*

He opened the front door carefully, and moving in a slightly erratic fashion to elude possible sniper's bullets, he retrieved his mail—quickly deadbolted the screen and main door once again, and re-armed the alarm.

He slipped on a pair of purple latex gloves, and then he passed the wand of his Geiger counter over the mail. No son-of-a-bitch was slipping *him* polonium-210.

He wanted to see a letter from Tabitha: her stern, hard-right-leaning handwriting. But there was just the usual credit card offers and coupons for Bangor Raceway.

He'd hoped to get his EZ-Pass receipt for the month and follow exactly where Tabby might have gone—spread out the map on the dining room floor and trace every Goddamn tollbooth and bridge she'd passed. There was no EZ-Pass receipt. Maybe he could request one online? Of course that would mean remembering his password—a complete impossibility now that he had 84 of them.

There was a package in the pile. The return address said Shoop. This was his crazy friend Kim who managed a bookstore somewhere in Pennsylvania. Inside the envelope he found a paperback called *Sex for One: The Joy of Selfloving*. A post-it note on the cover read: "Steve, I know you've got your hands full, but I hope you enjoy this. —Kimmy."

Thanks, Kim. Now I can spend *more* time jerking off. Or die trying. He flipped open the book and read the printed dedication: *This book is dedicated to me. Without my selflove it could never have been written.*

Now *this* was the kind of book he should have been writing. *Sixty Years of Jerking Off: A Memoir and a Box of Kleenex—with Special Companion DVD Featuring Kirsten Dunst Standing in the Rain in* Spiderman *with Digitally-Enhanced Nipples and Extended Author's Commentary Track.*

Thanks, Shoop. Thanks for reminding me I'm sitting alone in this house with nothing but a dusty storage drawer full of old *Hustlers*. Stroke books, Lenny Bruce had called them. He laughed as he imagined the magazine racks at Borders arranged alphabetically: *Arts, Entertainment, General Interest, Sports, Stroke.* Every rack is empty of customers except for a pack of 14-year-old boys with impenetrable eyeglasses gravely flipping through *Popular Beaver*.

His bill from Working Assets long distance was in the pile. *Yes, I rounded up!* read the checkbox on the bottom of the bill each month—and each month he defaced its cheerful progressivism in a new manner. Two months ago he'd written: *Yes, I rounded down!* And he happily shorted them 35 cents. Last month he'd written: *Yes, I rounded up, but then I thought better of it and withdrew my initial impulse towards generosity.* He hoped he was amusing some anonymous clerk at the processing center in Minnesota (some cool college girl named Shannon slumming for a semester while she finished her novel *Paint the Floor Yellow and Dance!*) In truth, he knew his editorializing on the bill was probably only bewildering some 300-pound Doofus McGoofus who stared at it for a minute and a half. "Dere's wriding on it." Some moron like the stupid fuck who ran him over.

This is a watchbird watching a FUCKING MORON. This is a watchbird watching YOU. Were you a FUCKING MORON today?

King's memory had drifted back to *Flock of Watchbirds*, a red hardback children's book by Munro Leaf he had owned as a child. The book, and its illustrations of red and black worried-looking birds, admonished children not to be a SMASHER, a THOUGHTLESS, a BED-BAWLER, A FOOD-FUSSER, or a LAZY. *This is a Lazy. It won't get up in the morning until somebody pulls it out of bed. Everybody forgot to pull this one, so it slept all through Christmas and didn't have any fun. Were you a LAZY today?*

A frowning figure with a red nose lay in bed, eyes closed, a Christmas tree lit in the background.

Fifty years ago and he remembered this.

He was still afraid of being a LAZY. That was probably why he wrote so much. Too Goddamned much. But maybe this was the one. Maybe *this* was the seventh wave.

He sat here writing books nobody gave a shit about. Even his agent had described *The Cell* as "compelling." What kind of lukewarm bullshit was that? *Compelling.* That meant: my assistant skimmed it. Can you write something a little more, I don't know, *contemporary*, Stephen?

Yeah, and can you suck my contemporary dick?

This is Stephen King, the guy who once walked with the wazmo.

This is a watchbird watching a LONELY.

This is a watchbird watching a PANICKED.

This is a watchbird watching a DESPERATE.

"Tabby, Tabby, Tabby"—her name poured out of his mouth.

Tabby, save me.

A fan of *The Green Mile* had sent him an antique electric chair that he kept in an unused corner of the living room. King sat in it now. The shadows of the barred picture window fell across him. He felt small and doomed. He continued to examine his mail. The second page of the Working Assets bill ($89.67 *No, I Didn't Fucking Round Up*) was Tabby's cell phone. Last call made August 8. Eight was a lucky numeral in Chinese mythology. All the new drivers in China were fighting to get 8's on their license plates. Three calls on August 8. All *incoming*. First call: one minute. 11:33 A.M. Second call: one minute. 12:01 P.M. Third call: 27 minutes. 2 P.M. He called the Working Assets "friendly customer service" number (800-362-7127) to see if there was any information on "incoming."

Yes, that information was on file. One moment while I bring it up.

"Am I speaking with Stephen King?" the male voice asked.

"That's my name."

"The writer Stephen King?"

"I'm his cousin."

"Oh. Well, if you talk to your cousin will you tell him how much I loved *The Stand*? I read the uncut version. It took me all summer long."

"Great."

"I loved it. But I was a little disappointed in the ending."

"You were a little disappointed."

"Yeah, all the evil people just get wiped out by

a nuclear missile. That just seemed to me, I don't know, so *convenient.*"

"Really?"

"Yeah, I mean, like, I read 900 pages and then it just ends like that? All that build-up about the big war between good and evil. You think there's going to be this enormous Armageddon scene. You know, this fantastic epic battle? And instead he just cops out and the evil people conveniently blow themselves up."

"What did you want me to do? Write *another* thousand pages?"

"I'm just saying I felt gypped at the end."

"And what am I supposed to do about it? Rewrite the fucking book?"

"Look, I'm just giving my opinion."

"Did I ask for your opinion? I asked where the fucking incoming calls are coming from."

"They came from 207-526..."

"Do you have a name for that number?"

"The computer says *unidentified.*"

"Where's the 526 exchange?"

Clicking of computer keys.

"Swan's Island Vicinity."

King wrote this down on the margin of the Working Assets bill.

"Hey, I'm sorry about not liking the end."

"You know what?" said King. "*You* write a better ending."

"I didn't say that—"

"And before you try that, you know what you can do? Try writing a better *paragraph.*"

"Look, Mr. King—"

"And before you do that, try writing a better *sentence* than me."

"I never said that—"

King hung up.

Don't lose your temper, Steve. He heard Tabitha's voice. *You just give them ammunition against you.*

She was right. She was always right.

He slipped his left wrist into the leather strap of the electric chair.

He rubbed his finger along the string of phone numbers she'd called. Nine tenths of them were to her girlfriend Katya in Camden, ME, Camden, ME, Camden, ME, Camden, ME. What the hell did they talk about every day?

Answer: *Him.*

They talked about what an insane, paranoid freak he was turning into, how she couldn't take one more minute in this madhouse.

Who on earth did she know on Swan's Island?

Bad place, said his unconscious.

He had never been there, but the island had the reputation of being slightly sinister. A 30-minute ferry ride from the shore of Mount Desert Island. The general vibe given off by the name Swan's Island was that of some aloof, wealthy, clannish bunch who *liked* being isolated; who discouraged visitors; who offered no amenities to people who felt inclined to take the ferry.

When precisely had she walked out? ("Stephen, you're just too crazy to live with. You want to write, and then you cut yourself completely off from the world? How fucked up is that?") He thought it may have been August 8.

She hadn't made a single call in three weeks?

Who was calling her for 27 minutes from Swan's Island?

Her lover.

Why hadn't there been any previous long calls on her cell phone record?

She'd been careful.

All those Goddamn calls to Camden! Maybe those weren't to Katya? Maybe Katya was electronically *forwarding* those calls to someone else. To Mr. Swan's Island Loverboy. Mr. White Wine and Polished Hardwood Dick.

He struggled to release himself from the electric chair, and he walked, almost blindly, into Tabby's office. Dark. Organized. Framed book jackets of *Small World*, *The Trap*, *Caretakers*, and *Grimoire*—her first book of poems. On the right-hand wall a framed review from *Publisher's Weekly* and a full-sized film poster for Truffaut's *Stolen Kisses*. The poster— tinted in red—was an extreme close-up photo of a woman's lips and teeth. Part of her nose was visible too. No eyes. It was, he thought, a highly erotic image, and he wondered what exactly was its appeal for women? Maybe it was like those Georgia O'Keeffe flowers that looked like vaginas. Maybe women just liked checking out vaginas. Maybe it was why they liked men with beards so much; all that hair around an open mouth; it was like talking to a vagina!

Maybe Tabby would come back if he regrew his beard.

Or if he wrote his novels in a suggestively revised typography:

> *Her*
> *Name*   *was*
> *Tabitha*   *but she*
> *Liked to call*   *herself Emma*
> *In impish*   *tribute to*
> *Flaubert's*   *masterpiece*
> *And in*   *some*   *slightly embarrassing*
> *Way she felt*   *a*   *spiritual kinship*
> *To that poor*   *sad*   *romantic spirit*
> *Suffocating in*   *that*   *poor sad town*
> *Drowning in*   *the*   *pettiness of the*
> *Bourgeoisie,*   *the*   *soullessness of the*
> *Middle class,*   *that barren,*
> *Suburban*   *desert of*
> *Philistines,*   *the hopelessly*
> *passionless*   *landscape of*
> *Bangor.*

Now *that* would get him on *Good Morning, America.* "Mr. King, your novel is just so *compelling*," Diane Sawyer would gush. "As a woman, I felt in looking at Emma that I was looking *exactly* at myself." Maybe he'd get it serialized in *Hustler*? Or *The Village Vomit*? He thought of that phrase he used to type at the top of his short stories when he first started submitting them: *First Serial Rights.* As if anybody, *anywhere* was interested in acquiring the rights to the titanic epics of garbage that were pouring out of him without cessation: secret agents trapped under mysterious hanging lamps that paralyzed only their *voluntary* nervous systems— so that the only way to escape was to vividly *imagine* intense physical activity. Then the agent's breath would slowly accelerate in microscopic increments until he could eventually *aim* his breath at the hanging lamp causing it to start moving like a pendulum. Tiny movements. Then longer and longer arcs of oscillation. The agent's breath fanned the movement. Every time the lamp momentarily swung its paralyzing beam away, his breath grew stronger, until, after five hours labor, the lamp had finally swung far away that his strength could return just long enough to sweep himself off the table—and escape!

This was a story he'd actually submitted to *The New Yorker* when he was a teenager.

He remembered that Sunday felt like the only genuinely restful day of the week for him because it was the one day he could receive no rejections—those 10x13 clasp envelopes that appeared in his mailbox every other morning.

Rejections from *Startling Mystery Stories*.

Somewhere in this house he still had the old yellow hardback with the black lettering: *Writer's Market 1970*. He'd read its pages as closely and as relentlessly as he'd read the Johnson Smith catalogue when he was 11 years old—when he'd spent a dollar for *Learn How to Be a Handcuff King and Mystery Man*. "Baffling tricks of mystery Worth Ten Dollars each to anyone making professional use of them."

And hadn't he grown up to be a Handcuff King and Mystery Man after all? Hadn't he spent his entire adult life offering to his readers baffling tricks of mystery? And then explained how the tricks were done? Given them a fantastic magic trick and then told them *exactly* how the trick was accomplished? There was no more powerful narrative than that.

His gaze returned to the *Stolen Kisses* poster of the woman's lips.... Tabitha had adored those old Truffaut movies. She'd cried when she'd read Truffaut's obituary in the *Bangor Daily News.* She owned all the DVDs; the boxed set of the Antoine Doinel films.

King himself had never much connected with those particular movies, but he loved that she loved them. He admired her passion; he admired her intelligence; her sense of satire. They played this game drawn from the end of an episode of *The Avengers* she loved: "The Joker." Emma Peel had been terrorized by an escaped madman in an old house. To the music of an ancient 78 r.p.m. record—"Mein Liebling, Mein Rose"—dapper John Steed rescued her by hitting the madman on the head with a gigantic playing card!

When King would arrive home now from even a five-minute trip downtown, Tabby, as Emma, would sigh and say: "Stephen...It's been quite a night...." And he, as John Steed, the poised and elegant rescuer, would reply: "Well, it's morning now...the fog's lifted...let's get a breath of fresh air."

Christ, he didn't even know who Truffaut *was* until he'd met her. He was too busy staying up till 2 A.M. to watch WAGM play *Motel Hell* on Creature Features. She'd taught him about Seymour Glass; she'd taught him about Paul Simon. They used to sing to each other that lost song that Simon had once performed on *The Dick Cavett Show*:

Let me live in your city,
The rivers are pretty,
I'm just a traveler,
Eatin' up my travelin' time.

He looked at her wooden caseful of CDs. All that wonderfully embarrassing material from the early days. *The Vanilla Fudge: The Beat Goes On!*

When the world was young.

They were delightfully absurd memories—and absolutely meaningless without her.

Mein liebling, mein rose.

"It's been quite a night."

"Well, it's morning now...the fog's lifted...let's get a breath of fresh air."

The late morning sun through the budding maple trees cast undulating shadows of the barred windows across the entire room. The shadows were moving all around him— even on the ceiling. It was *The Day of the Triffids* and the vines were closing in on him. It was all the more terrifying because it was silent. Something out there was trying to get in. If it couldn't get in through the barred windows it would get in through—

The telephone rang.

The private line.

He let it ring four times, then he picked up.

"Stephen! This is Tom Clancy!"

The connection was bad—a cell-phone call dipping in and out of existence.

"Stephen, I think somebody is trying to kill..."

And then the call turned to static; became clear for one more second; he heard Clancy's voice shouting *representative!* and then there was silence.

The shadows of the barred windows pulsed around him. A net was closing in on him. He felt he couldn't breathe.

He had to do what he feared the most.

He had to leave his house.

He pressed the garage door opener and rolled back out into the driveway. He was driving his vintage black hearse painted with *The Prisoners* on the side. It had apparently once belonged to an old rock band, and the graphic on the doors showed the four faces of the band members standing behind bars, before a Graustarkian setting, in a manner reminiscent of the final image of the old *Prisoner* television series.

BNGRBRNT.

He could hear the hearse's heavy tires rolling down the macadam.

The electronic gate at the end of the driveway squealed open: a noisy, rusty cry that told him with absolute certainly that this was the last car trip he would ever make.

As his car pulled onto West Broadway, he realized he didn't even know where he was heading.

Never coming home, the electronic gate said as it locked back shut behind him.

His hands were visibly shaking.

He thought of Tabitha's last phone call.

Swan's Island.

FIVE

THE BIG
BOW-WOW
STUFF...

Tom Clancy was listening to Jerry Orbach singing "Try to Remember" from the original cast album of *The Fantasticks*. As Orbach sang *Try to remember/when life was so tender/that love was an ember/about to billow*, Clancy burst into tears.

His writing desk looked out onto the bay. On the corner of his desk a small color television was tuned to Fox News with the sound muted. Closed captioning appeared on the bottom of the screen.

The colors of the bay looked distorted through his blue sunglasses. Particularly the white pebbles of the beach seemed magnified in their whiteness; the brown stones surrounding them appeared gray.

Breaking news read the legend on the television, but Clancy was only half-conscious of it. He held a miniature wireless phone to this right ear, but he was barely aware of that either. His mind was deep in some other place: a room with no windows. A room with two long wooden tables. Six chairs at each table: each station equipped with an 8-inch PVM-9L3 hi-res monitor, a brass banker's lamp, and a telephone. Both the audio and video were banked into what some might have thought were standard RG1180 cables leading into what looked like a closet. In that temperature and humidity-sensitive closet stood a desk, an ergonomically correct business chair, and a large glass-enclosed rack containing what some might have thought were standard computer drives. In fact, they housed the most sensitive and complex encryption software that the mind of man and 32 billion dollars were capable of generating. Only four people on the planet understood the exact nature of the algorithms behind the software and how vital it might be if the President of the United States (POTUS) were required to orchestrate a war from this windowless room in the bunker behind his ranch. These four people were: Varun Singh, a scientist at MIT who had dreamed up the breakthrough per-bit-encoding paradigm that had created project MANGO LASSI COME HOME; two scientists from the Triptych Lab at Langley; and Jack Ryan, Jr.

Your call is important to Verizon and may be monitored for quality-control purposes. Please stay on the line. Clancy's phone continued to offer classical music interspersed with commercials about low-cost DSL.

"Representative!" yelled Clancy into the phone.

Still the music played.

"Representative!" he repeated.

He knew that Verizon's standard commercial 6SJ7GT voice-recognition preferences were keyed to allow a screaming customer *(I want to talk to a human being! I want to talk to a customer representative!)* to bypass the automated telephony and step to the rear of the electronic queue waiting for the one overworked actual human being in the building.

"Representative!"

Finally a click. The music ended and was replaced by an electronic internal ringing. Then: "Verizon Probem Resolution Center. Scarlett speaking. How may we help you this morning?"

"Listen, Scarlett," said Clancy. "I'm calling about noise on the line. Can you hear that? This phone has been virtually unusable for a week. A week which I'm sure you're billing me for. Now this is the *seventh* call I've made about this. And the problem is *not* the phone. Okay? I went out to the interface box and tested it. The problem is on the line. It's a *line* problem."

"I'm very sorry to hear that you're still having—"

"Look, Scarlett. Can I ask you something? Where are you located?"

A short pause, then: "This is the Verizon Problem Resolution Center."

"Yeah, I know that, Scarlett. But what I want to know is: where are you? Are you in America?"

"Sir, this is the Verizon Problem—"

"Are you in India?"

"Sir, I am authorized to—"

"Are you in India? Yes or no?"

"…Yes, sir, I am in India."

"You're an Indian named Scarlett?"

"Scarlett is not my real name."

"What is your real name?"

"…Deepa."

"Okay, Deepa, look, I've got no problem with *you*. I'm sure you're just a decent young woman trying to make a living. Fine. That's the American way. The Bombay way. Whatever. But I also know that there's only so much you can do: you've got to follow the script, right? Check off the little boxes on your computer screen? Try to get through as many customers as you can in an hour so your tally sheets look good? Okay, fine. I understand that. But the problem is that I've been through six Deepas already, okay? I've *heard* the script. And the problem is still not resolved. Can you hear that noise? I can barely hear you."

"Sir, I—"

"Look, Deepa, sweetheart. I want you to connect me with your supervisor in *America*, okay? Again, I've got nothing against you or your country. I love vegetable samosas. But I want to talk to somebody in *America*."

"One moment. I'm going to put you on hold for one minute."

"Don't put me on hold."

"For one minute, sir, and then I'm going to transfer you to a—"

"Don't put me on—"

Click. Then the Mozart started again.

"Representative! *Representative!*"

His eyes, by this point, had connected with the breaking news on Fox. There was a black and white photograph of film director François Truffaut looking about twenty years old, cigarette in hand, sitting at a table with Alfred Hitchcock whose left hand was raised in a demonstration of some cinematic point. Then the news cut to footage of an antique-looking cemetery where some kind of exhumation was taking place. Clancy turned up the sound.

"...the body of legendary New Wave film director François Truffaut was believed to be buried. Plans had been made to move his remains to a special memorial outside the Cinémathèque française at the Palais de Chaillot, across the river from the Eiffel Tower, the monument Truffaut loved so much. Truffaut had paid tribute to the Cinémathèque in this famous opening shot from his 1969 feature *Stolen Kisses*."

They cut to a film: Charles Trenet singing *"Que reste t-il de nos amours"* and a shot of a suburban park panned left to reveal the twin staircases leading down to the doors of the Cinémathèque française. A notice on the door, written in French, advised visitors that the museum was locked shut until further notice—a political reference to the Henri Langois affair of the period. "However," continued the reporter, "French authorities were astounded to discover that the remains of Truffaut, who was buried here in the Cimetière de Montmartre in 1984 had, apparently, been stolen." The visuals now showed a construction crane, a priest, and a group of policemen at the cemetery. "In a bizarre twist that might have been drawn from the master of suspense himself—" And here the news cut to Simon Oakland, as the psychiatrist at the conclusion of *Psycho*, saying: "A weighted coffin had been buried."

Clancy switched the sound to mute once again, and he pressed play on his CD player. A piano, a harp, a bass. And then there was the young Jerry Orbach singing: *Try to remember a time in September....*

He tried to return to his novel on the computer screen. His eyes moved to the sign he had mounted above his desk for inspiration: *How Would Lustbader Do It?* The phone remained jammed to his ear.

This was the novel, he thought, which not only would cement his reputation as a greater political writer than John le Carré but might also secure him an actual position on the President's cabinet. This novel was going to change international politics and international warfare. The title, he thought, would be *Mission Impossible: Accomplished!* The conceit of the novel was a precise outline for the way the wars in Iraq and Afghanistan *should* have been fought and won. It would be a meticulously accurate blueprint. The timetables. The troop deployments. The securing of the Pakistani border. Exact details. Precise numbers. The roadmap that *should* have been followed. Situation-room planners at the Pentagon would be passing this manuscript around (all 1,911 pages of it) as if it were the Holy Grail. Senators would be quoting it from the floor. Hugo Chavez would be handing out free copies on the streets of New Orleans along with Tupperware containers of home heating oil. It would be serialized in *Jane's Defense Monthly*. And, finally, the President would make the call. Leaning into his custom-made chair whose back was reinforced with sheets of Dupont Kevlar as additional reinforcement against bullets that might make it through the thick windows of lenticular polycarbonate that prismed the light from the lawn, the President would call him personally. "Tommy, I was wondering if we could talk. Just you and me."

It would be the natural culmination of 25 million books in print....

Clancy sighed. Then he signed onto Amazon.com and wrote yet another excoriation of John le Carré's *The Mission Song*.

HEZBOLLAPOPPIN! *

Reviewer: Makdi-El Sadr (East of the Sunni and West of the Mosque)

Maybe I'm just a radical cleric with my head up my girlfriend's burqa, but would somebody tell me just what the hell this incomprehensible rubbish is all about? Le Carré, for all his lit'ry pretensions, could take a couple of lessons from Tom Clancy in How to Just Tell a Story! I only wish I could give this book NO stars. And could somebody at Little Brown spend the money to hire a decent copy-editor? Hello! You don't spell "color" with a "u"! (p.101)

It was now 10 A.M., and he switched the CD player over to WOMR (Outer Cape Radio 87.1 FM) which was broadcasting *Democracy Now!*

From the radio Amy Goodman announced: "From Pacifica, this is *Democracy Now!*" Then a reporter's voice translating from Lebanese: "Last night we heard Israeli planes flying over us. We were about 50 people in the room, about 30 children…Most of the children died." Amy Goodman spoke: "The Qana killings. The world's called on the UN to investigate the Israeli government for war crimes…And part two of our interview with Mohammed Mahtzo Miehle, author of *Enema Combatant: My High-Colonic Interrogation at Guantánamo….*"

He listened to this show because it infuriated him with its simplistic sloganeering and its knee-jerk liberalism: Oh, yeah, let's *negotiate* with the jihadists—let's sit down and *interview* the people who blew up the wedding reception— the people refilling their bottles of Aussie Three-Minute Miracle with something from the *Anarchist's Cookbook* to blow up an entire airplane full of students. Yeah, Amy, how many *funerals* did you go to today? Or were you too busy submitting dubs of your pieces for the Peabodys?

It made him so furious he actually had to pace the room while he listened.

The phone rang.

"Mr. Clancy—"

The phone line was absolutely noiseless.

"Hey, Verizon, thank God you fixed the—"

His voice trailed away because suddenly and intuitively he knew it was not the phone company on the other end of his tiny wireless phone.

"If you value your life," said a male voice, "you'll be at the top of the monument tonight at midnight."

"Who is this?"

"And, Mr. Clancy? This call may be monitored for quality control."

The noise of the phone line returned. The call was over.

Clancy stood with a feeling rising in his throat that was equal parts panic and fury.

...the top of the monument tonight at midnight...

He turned around and incoherently took in the details of this one room on the second floor of his vacation home. It had always felt like a monastic retreat: a desk, a bed, a tiny kitchenette, a smoky brick fireplace, a couch, a throw-rug, a framed enlargement of the cover of *Tom Clancy's Executive Bathroom*, a stall shower filled with spiders, old sagging book-shelves and citronella candles.

Its previous owner had been the writer A.H.Z. Carr, and the shelves were still full of musty paperbacks that must have once been of use to him: *Italian by This Rapid System Without a Teacher* by A. Vavolizza, published by Authentic Publications. Aging magazines that had once printed his stories: *Ellery Queen's Mystery Magazine, July 50¢ 1964. 32 Extra Pages. New Short Novel—Complete! A.H.Z. Carr The Washington Party Murder—about the mysterious death of a famous political columnist...set against the V.I.P. social life of Washington—senators, generals, diplomats—and gossip!*

Clancy's head was spinning, and he lay down on the folded pink bedspread. Amy Goodman's voice continued to hammer out the headlines.

Another writer?

Another death?

Hadn't he secretly known the next victim would be he?

Who else *could* it be?

If they were killing the most bankable writers in the world, who else could they choose? John le Carré? Christ, the guy hadn't written a readable novel since *Tinker, Tailor*. And *that* book was 200 pages too long. Let's face it, the guy hadn't written a decent piece of fiction since *The Spy Who Came in From the Cold.*

What monument? he suddenly thought. Was he supposed to travel to D.C. by midnight and show up at the Washington monument? To hang out in the park with the homeless? To have his throat slit by a crack addict as he *waited* to be murdered by the Butcher of the Best Sellers.

He'd been reading the papers.

Sue Grafton, Danielle Steel, Curtis-what-the-fuck-was-her-name?

Somebody *seriously* did not like writers. And those were the bullshit writers. Now the killer was moving onto the heavies like Clancy. Why *didn't* they kill le Carré for Christ's sake? Just for fucking target practice. The guy probably listened to *Democracy Now!*

Criticizers! Satirists! Choking on their own insufferable self-congratulatory irony. You wanted to throw up. Al Franken, Noam Chomsky, Michael Moore, and the most criminally dangerous writer on the face of the earth today, Frank Rich. Not only should the President sue the *Times* for leaking the story about data collection by the phone companies (*"Representative!"*), he should sue the *Times* for publishing fucking Frank Rich. Put that guy back in Arts and Leisure! Let him spend his time happily reviewing *Yo Momma! Yo-Yo-Ma Plays the Great Rap Hits.* But keep him out of politics. No wonder Mel Gibson said the Jews caused all the wars. It was the Jewish writers like Rich who stirred up the trouble. And Jewish editors. And Jewish publishers. The whole *misbucha!* He didn't want to sound like Borat, but his next book, Clancy thought, would expose the entire Zionist media conspiracy...working title: *Circumcypto.* (Jerry Goniff of Posthumous Press had told him he *loved* the concept when they spoke last year at the Buchenwald Book Fair.)

Clancy adjusted his blue sunglasses and zipped up his red windbreaker with *U.S.S. Depleted Uranium* stitched on the front and an American flag on the back bearing the legend: *These colors don't have a radioactive half-life of 100,000 years!*

He glanced at the clock as he switched off Amy Goodman. It was noon. He heard that unsettling voice again in his head: "If you value your life, you'll be at the top of the monument tonight at midnight."

That was 12 hours from now.

Clancy, if these actually were the last 12 hours of your life, how differently would you view the world?

What had Jimmy Stewart said in *Mr. Smith Goes to Washington*? "Try to live life as if you just came out of a tunnel...."

He would go to the police.

In every novel Miss Plausible always asked, "Why don't we go to the police?" And Mr. Extended Chase Sequence inevitably replied, "They'd never believe us." But, in this case, Clancy was determined to bring the authorities immediately into the loop. They knew Clancy; they loved his books. They were going to let him die on their watch?

He twisted the two Medico titanium locks that guarded his upstairs lair and descended the wooden staircase on the side of the house. He held tightly to the rail in case one of the steps had been sawn in half, then lightly glued back in place by the killer.

The first floor of his house was unoccupied at the moment. In a few weeks his wife Alexandra would join him. But for now she was busy bombing stem-cell research centers. Clancy himself had taught her the tradecraft: purified ammonia nitrate detonated with a cesium spark by a cell-phone trigger. It was true that some lab workers had been seriously injured during her last intervention, but Clancy consoled her with the thought of the number of frozen embryos they'd managed to save. (*Wake Up America, The Embryos are Defrosting!*)

As he descended the cedar steps he wondered if these, in fact, *were* the final twelve hours in his life. What if *Mission Impossible: Accomplished!* was never completed? He half-hoped it might be remembered as his unfinished masterpiece...his *The Mystery of Edwin Drood*. And what if *Circumcypto* was never begun? He'd die like Flaubert, approaching the finish line of *Bouvard and Pécuchet*, but never actually crossing over. So, okay, Tom Clancy hadn't exactly been acclaimed by the French Legion of Honor, but Clancy certainly understood the world being parodied in *Madame Bovary*. When Flaubert mocked the hypocrisy of the philistine bourgeoisie, Clancy felt it resonated exactly with the self-satisfied fraudulence of the liberals and progressives who moved around him now down Bang Street—aliens—these politically enlightened hordes with their ipods and college sweatshirts and gelled hair and high-season suntans and purple flip-flops and self-adoring smiles that said: I-only-shave-on-Wednesdays-and-I'm-too-fucking-cool-to-tuck-my-shirt-in. They sat with their wireless laptops on public benches conducting their conspicuously *urgent* business so we all had to see.

He moved onto Commercial Street. The traffic and the noise increased: the 1980s music from the juice bar, the muscleman in his ball cap with his miniature bulldog trotting without a leash two feet behind him—the muscleman too *progressive* to actually turn his head to check whether his dog had been run over by the Mercedes Cab Company. No, thought, Clancy, our muscleman was too *enlightened* for that...it was the *cab's* fault, not his own stupid self-absorbed indifference. Then there was the long-haired woman in the peasant dress playing a full-sized gold-painted harp in front of the library—and the tourist shop with its pornographic bumper stickers in the twirling racks: *The Itty Bitty Titty Club* and *Bush Happens.* And the keychains with Bush's picture and *Days Remaining* electronically counting down. This was the President for Christ's sake! What other country would tolerate this kind of open derision?

He thought: *As a child I venerated the President.* He still venerated the President—it wasn't the specific man, it was the chain of command. You didn't criticize your commanding officer. You closed ranks. That was biggest lesson the *progressives* needed to learn: to shut the fuck up. Right or wrong, that was the way an organization worked; the way a country worked. You delegated authority to a soldier, a cop, a senior officer—then you got out of the fucking way and let him do his job, unimpeded by this endless barrage of micro-management and second-guessing and protest rallies.

He adjusted his aviator sunglasses as he stormed west on Commercial Street. Just look at fucking South America! Three hundred years of political protests and marching on the capital and Che Guevara t-shirts and what did they have to show for it? An entire continent whose average individual income was 38 *centavos.* A populace that still drove 1955 Buicks and lived in cinderblock slums. One more assassination. One more political coup. One more fascist strongman who six months later would be bleeding in *el camino* with 267 shells in his body. Long live *la libertad*! Now let's all get together and interview the *new* Fascist leader at the *fiesta del Amy Goodman!* And, hey, while we've got you all here, let's protest animal testing, clitorectomies, and The Gap!

He stopped at a pay phone by the wharf and punched in the number of his credit card. The sun glinted hard off the bright white hulls of the Dolphin whale-watching fleet. When the dial tone emerged he dialed Stephen King's number in Bangor. A pause. Then a thin, distant ringing.

"Stephen, this is Tom Clancy. I think someone is trying to kill me."

The signal cut off.

Somebody's monitoring my calls. Even my payphone calls.

The tourists and the locals swarmed around him as he moved into the West End: the freaks, the sickos, the trannis, the fucking liberals. Next stop: the collapse of civilization. The elevator had descended as low as it could possibly go: Depravityville. They smelled of Neutrogena sunblock and too many hours with nothing to do. He hated their immaculately white teeth. He hated their blue eyes. He hated their ice cream cones.

He walked into the bookstore and without hesitation found the store's one copy of John le Carré's *The Mission Song* in the new fiction section. What had Michiko Kakutani called it? A "highly simplistic, black-and-white thriller"? A "static talkfest"? God bless her. He'd sent thirty-five dollars to the *Times* Neediest Cases Fund as a reward for her bad review. He sent another hundred when she panned the Pynchon.

He turned the le Carré novel around backwards so the spine was no longer visible—beautifully hidden between part four of Bob Woodward's Iraq trilogy (*Bush: Moron or What?*) and the Imus biography (*'Tis a Pity She's a Ho*).

Clancy continued his walk, almost blindly. He turned right down a narrow street and headed directly into the Château de Vincennes, a dingy, half-collapsed white-framed two-storey building across the street from the Atlantic House. It had been a failed bed-and-breakfast, a failed art gallery, and a failed dinner theatre.

Clancy needed to punch a three-digit security code into the lock just to gain admittance into the foyer. In a white wooden booth where, no doubt, a mincing maître d' had once surveyed the scene, there now stood a deeply tanned and well-toned blonde young man dressed only in a black Speedo and a considerable amount of make-up. The Speedo was decorated with a red M&M saying: *Melts in your mouth, not in your hand.*

"It's getting hot out there, isn't it?" said the young man cheerily.

Clancy stared at him with what he hoped was icy contempt.

"Name?" sighed the young man.

"Flaubert."

The young man entered the name into his computer. "We got two Flauberts. Gustave and Xena."

"Gustave."

"Go right upstairs, Gustave. *Mi casa es su casa.*" He gave a little hand gesture which said: *Whatever.*

"Do I get a hood?" asked Clancy.

The young man looked into a bin under the desk. "I've got red, black, or American flag."

"Black. I believe you have my script on file."

"What's it called?" asked the young man, ineffably bored.

"Conscience of a Conservative."

Twenty minutes later, wearing only a black leather hood, Tom Clancy stood with his wrists handcuffed to an old iron hot-water radiator. The windows of the small, second-floor room were painted black, but the paint was thin and streaky, and the afternoon sun of Provincetown still managed to fill the room with a dim, watery, unpleasant light. There was funeral music leaking in from the room next door.

A smallish figure dressed head-to-toe in a spiked black leather body suit was spanking Clancy with a metal-spiked wooden bat. The figure's voice sounded as if it still hadn't broken, and Clancy figured he was probably underage. But at least he had a Goddamn strong hand.

"What's your name again?" Clancy asked.

"AC/DC."

"You're using my script, right?"

"I'm all over it."

"Can I ask you something?" said Clancy, trying to wipe the sweat from his eyes. "What's with the funeral music?"

"That's the room next door. It's got a coffin in it for guys who want to pretend they're fucking a corpse."

"...okay."

"Some guys are into some weird shit."

Clancy considered this. "Sounds like a lousy gig for the guy pretending to be the corpse."

"Actually it's not that bad. You get to *sleep* through most of it. You don't have to pretend, like, you're all *into* it and everything. I mean, you're *supposed* to be dead, right?"

"Let's start."

The leather figure looked at the well-creased script Clancy kept on file. He cleared his throat and said, "You're the Conservative, right?"

"Right."

"Okay." The boy suddenly read angrily and dramatically. "You lying piece of Conservative shit!"

Whack!

"You need to be *punished*, don't you, you fucking signee for the Committee for the New American Century? You scum-sucking Paul Wolfowitz-wannabe!"

Whack!

"I'm sorry," said Clancy.

"Sorry! Sorry doesn't cut it, Mr. We'll-Be-Greeted-As-Liberators!"

Whack!

"I'm sorry. I went by the best intelligence I was given."

"Mr. We'll-Be-Greeted-with-Flowers?"

Whack!

"I didn't *know*."

"Saddam had 45 tons of anthrax? Where? Up his asshole?"

Whack!

"Tenet said it was a slam-dunk."

"You wanna know what a slam-dunk feels like, you Fox-News-watching war criminal?"

Whack! Whack!

"Three thousand Americans dead and how many more wounded, you Family-Values-spouting, gay-bashing, worthless piece of shit?"

Whack! Whack! Whack!

"Please stop," said Clancy.

"Why don't you beg like you made them beg at Guantanemo when they tied them to the waterboard."

"We never authorized that."

"Well, did you authorize *this*, you fucking rewriter of the Geneva Convention?"

Whack! Whack! Whack! Whack!

At the end of the session, the figure unlocked Clancy's hands. Clancy was bruised and sweaty.

"You did good," said Clancy. He meant it as legitimate praise.

"It's not hard when the writing's good," said the figure, who pulled off her hood and shook down her long blonde hair.

She smiled at Clancy.

He recognized her immediately.

It was Ann Coulter.

"A.C. from D.C," Clancy said.

She nodded and smiled.

"You want to get something to eat?" asked Clancy.

"Sorry. I gotta another client in, like, five minutes."

"Anybody I know?"

She lowered her voice to a whisper. "Trent Lott."

"Wow. What is *that* like?"

"All I'll say is that *he* wears the dildo."

Clancy felt less furious when he left the Château de Vincennes, but he did not feel substantially less frightened. If this did turn out to be the last day of his life, he'd at least spent his final few hours meaningfully.

He walked down Shank Panter Road and passed some time in conference with the Provincetown Police Department. With their bright yellow short-sleeved shirts and black plastic bicycle helmets, he thought he might as well be asking for protection from the Muppets. ("Let's all hold each other's hands, sing the *Fraggle Rock* song, and *strongly visualize* the bad guys melting into brown sugar! Okay, guys!")

Still, they assured him they would guard Pilgrim Monument from the moment it closed at three. (And, really, what other monument could it be?) They would maintain an armed vigil there all night long—with a break at 7:30 p.m., of course, to see the revival of Charles Ludlam's *Camille* at the

New Provincetown Playhouse—this is the *last* night it's playing—have you seen it yet, Tom? Oh, God, it's a *riot*....

They would leave the monument unlocked at midnight so he could ascend its 116 stone steps. Inside there would be two more policemen hidden at the top.

He killed some time at a vegetarian restaurant he liked: Tofu A Go-Go. The place wasn't really open after 9 P.M. but Simôn, the woman who worked there, with her crew cut and her nose ring, loved his novels. This is my audience, he thought: tough-ass diesel dykes who can cook a killer whole-wheat burrito. Maybe he *should* stop writing. Spend the remainder of his days licensing his videogames: Tom Clancy's *Kick My Conservative Ass With a Spiked Bat!* Not recommended for conservatives under nine.

One of the best things about Tofu A Go-Go was that it was located on an open-air second floor porch, and if you sat near the railing you could watch, almost entirely unobserved, the passing parade down below on Commercial Street. The vision of strollers and roller-skaters and—what was it, yearning?—struck him this night as both ludicrous and impossibly fragile. *Impossibly fragile* was not a phrase that frequently came to his lips. *M29 with Gemtech HALO suppressor* was a more likely phrase. But tonight there it was... marching beneath him: the water bottles, the pale legs, the leaflets for Varla Jean Merman...*impossibly fragile.* Maybe a threat on your life did that. Either it was the imminent possibility of death that was making him reflective or else it was getting spanked by Ann Coulter while handcuffed to a radiator. God, life was bizarre. The temptation to escape beckoned at every turning. What were those endless chases he'd written over and over again but a passion to escape? And who was Jack Ryan if he wasn't the version of Tom Clancy who finally made it over the wall—the wall of caution, responsibility, obligation, predictability. No wonder they pre-ordered his books.

Tom, give me a twenty-hour reprieve from my life as assistant service manager at Hyannis Honda. Let me disappear into your book.

Marine Specialties was Clancy's favorite store in Provincetown: an arcane and odoriferous junkshop of old bells, buoys, diving suits, and barrels of useless but deeply appealing military surplus material. There were piles of gasmasks in which German soldiers probably died sixty years earlier; there were barrels of military hats and soldiers' stripes, embossed police badges in unpronounceable languages, metal army hats painted bright blue with a soldier's name still inked on the chin-strap, boxes of Doc Marten shoes in sizes nobody wanted, marbles, reading glasses for $1.98, trashcans full of black "nylon police batons"—both the half-size and the full brain-bludgeoning size. There were ancient first-aid kits. There were pale orange tank tops with Marine Specialties stenciled in white. Rainbow feathered boas. A life preserver. A diving suit. An upright piano.

In the back, in the glass cases, was the genuinely wicked-looking weaponry: black-bladed Malayan kriss-knives shaped like the letter S; foldable blackjacks; ruby-handled balance knives with serrated edges like hacksaw blades; foot-long switchblades; and the Liberian nickel-handled blood knife shaped like a 3-inch-wide corkscrew to tear out an opponent's still-warm heart.

Clancy, perhaps indefensibly, bought nearly every one of these implements of intimate combat, and he spent his final hours before midnight in his garage, strapping them onto his belt, his leg, his forearm, his back. He thought if he walked into airport security right now the X-ray machine would have a coronary. He duct-taped two more knives to his calves. He hung the Liberian blood knife to a hook fitted on his belt. He put a CR123 three-volt lithium battery into his D-321B Generation 3 Grade-A Dual-Tube night-vision binoculars. With the strap around his neck, he kept the binoculars hidden under his windbreaker. *Look like a tourist,* he told himself. Like a big, dumb slightly-lost tourist who'd just parked his out-of-state S.U.V. in the Duarte parking lot— four dollars for the first three hours, payable in advance.

It was 11 o'clock.

The police had lent him one of their walkie-talkies. Clancy had laughed. It was a cheap, unscrambled Motorola X11; the kind of thing you'd pick up on the clearance table at Radio Shack. He shook his head as it beeped on in a cough of loud static. Any idiot with a scanner could intercept the signal. Christ, he was being protected by Toys R Us. The Provincetown Police Department—brought to you by Mattel. They probably brought down assailants with SuperSoakers:

"Stop or I'll get you wet!"

"Okay, I give up! Just don't get water on the suede, all right?"

"Is that real suede?"

"Yes."

"God, I've never seen that *color* before."

These were the guys who were going to save him. Jesus, you might as well call in the Brownies.

Clancy clanked down Bradford Street, past the post office and the new theatre and the bed-and-breakfasts with *Pet Friendly* hanging below their signs. They all had names with "snug" and "cozy" in them. When he imagined the fantastic carnal dissipation going on behind those snug, cozy walls, he thought more appropriate names might be Chez

Auto-Asphyxiation or Ye Olde Flaming Anus 'n' Andy Inn. *Clank. Clank. Clank.* Knives and nylon police baton and night goggles created a ludicrous percussion-track as he walked. He was half-man, half-weaponry. Robot Commando in his red windbreaker and his *U.S.S. Reluctant* ball cap given to him by Stephen King who knew how much he admired *Mr. Roberts.* Not the movie! The short stories. He still cried when Ensign Pulver got that last letter from Roberts—and then the telegram that Roberts had been killed—not even fighting— the roof had fallen in on him. Collateral damage. It was one of those moments of plain, pure truth. The inarticulateness of genuine pain. Tom Heggen had captured it at age 25, a year or two before he killed himself, poor bastard. Tom Clancy had never been able to capture it. No, he clanked and he thumped and he thundered. As Sir Walter Scott had written about Jane Austen: *The Big Bow-Wow strain I can do myself like any now going; but the exquisite touch, which renders ordinary commonplace things and characters interesting, from the truth of the description and the sentiment, is denied to me.* The Big Bow-Wow stuff Clancy *could* do: the high-tech weaponry he'd carefully culled from *Jane's Defense Weekly.* But the private pain that Heggen effortlessly managed to wring from the poor, hopeless, *offstage* death of Lt. (j.g.) Douglas A. Roberts—that kind of poetry had forever eluded Clancy. It had eluded him despite the 800-page big, booming, bow-wow behemoths he'd birthed. *Maybe* he'd nail it this time, in *Mission Impossible: Accomplished!* A scene near the end. Jack Ryan, Jr. dies *offstage.* His bosom buddy, Lt. (j.g.) Buddy Bosun, reads the *we regret to inform you* letter. (Note to self: set up buddy character.) But Jack Ryan, Jr. was a loner. That was his greatness. Okay, so the buddy character has a buddy—and *that* guy gets killed. Or *almost* gets killed. Jack Ryan, Jr. saves them all in this fantastic finale sequence with machine guns blazing—and maybe a helicopter. *Hanging* from a helicopter with a machine gun! Damn, this was getting good. Fuck *Mr. Roberts.*

Clancy had the image in his mind's eye of a man dressed in traditional Arab garb with a machine gun in his hand—spraying everyone around him—when suddenly he stopped dead in the street. Directly across the street from Lemba's Health Foods. He would remember this place. Remember this moment when he had his greatest story idea ever: the story he'd be remembered for.

He closed his eyes and could hear himself breathing. Could hear the insane trilling of the crickets.

The image became clearer: the man in the Arab garb was Jack Ryan, Jr. His face had been painted in make-up to give him a Mid-Eastern appearance. (Jimmy Stewart and that guy on the bus in *The Man Who Knew Too Much*?) Up from his tarboosh he draws his machine gun—already firing 3.5 bullets per second. Spraying the entire table—

—it's the *Last Supper*—

Jack Ryan, Jr. has been sent back in time to stop the crucifixion of Jesus.

Damn, this was going to be bigger than the *DaVinci Code.*

Ryan has been sent through the time machine back to Bethlehem. He abducts Jesus on the street—pulls him into a wine shop, shakes him by the neck of his robe and tries to explain to him what's going to happen.

"Look, I'm Jack Ryan, Jr.! I'm from the future! Believe me! You're going to die tomorrow!"

Jesus looks up at him. He's got the saddest brown eyes the world has ever seen. Doomed eyes that understand the hurt even before the deathblow. "Of course I'm going to die tomorrow," Jesus says quietly. "Do you think I don't know that?"

"Listen! You can't die! Not this time."

"Don't you see? I *have* to die."

"Oh, shut the fuck up, will you?"

Jack pulls him into the alley and injects him. ("Heavenly father, forgive me for anaesthetizing your son. I swear it's only temporary. Believe me, Jews are going to be doing this *every* day in the future.") Jack's henchmen stow Jesus away in the basement of a local synagogue.

Meantime, Jack darkens his face, puts in brown contacts, and attaches a false beard to look like Him. He finds a mezuzah someplace. He wears Jesus's robe and walks slowly and spiritually through the streets. Beggars come up and ask him holy questions: "Tell me, Jesus, is there a proper blessing for the Czar?"

Then: Last Supper Time with Ryan at the center of the table disguised as the Prince of Peace.

Clinking of the wine cups. Tableful of lamb and matzoh and freshly ground horseradish. "Phew!" says Peter. "This stuff opened my sinuses right up." His partner Paul is trying to get disciples to invest in his new product: "I'm thinking of calling it Almond Joy?"

"It's no halvah, I can tell you that."

Ryan stands and solemnly intones. "One of you is going to betray me."

There is a stunned silence at the Seder table.

His accusation hangs in the air as an unassailable indictment.

"And..." continues Ryan, "I'm not waiting around to find out who the fuck it is!" He whips his machine gun out from under his robes—and the table explodes in gunfire and gefilte fish. Wine cups fly, crockery smashes. White robes darken with blood.

"All I said was that it was no halvah—" begins a disciple, but his sentence is stopped in a checkerboard of blood-hits across his face.

Screams of the dying.

Blood pouring. Wine dripping. The air is hot and dusty with smashed wood and the smell of cordite.

Smoke clearing over this slaughterhouse as Ryan stands in the middle of the table with his AK47 still loaded. Everyone else is dead or dying.

Freeze frame.

That's the cover of the book, thought Clancy.

Working title: *Thirty Seconds Over Bethlehem.*

Make Your Reservation for the Very Last Supper.

He'd call Spielberg about it in the morning. Of course, he'd read Spielberg was busy at the moment with his own revenge drama *What Price Waterhouse?*—the story of a fictional film director who systematically kills every one of the Academy voters because they didn't give him the Oscar for *Munich.*

Clancy's walkie-talkie crackled to life, breaking his reverie.

"All players in final position. TomCat, what is your location?"

Beep.

Clancy spoke into the unit. "This is TomCat. Location: 1,000 feet from target."

The target was Pilgrim Monument which was dramatically lit from below. There were 500 feet of dense forest all around it: chain-linked and barbed wired to keep out the roaming bands of teenagers with their trail bikes, headbands, and cell-phones. The exit driveway to the monument was on a dead dark street called High Pole Hill, and it looked perilously dark to Clancy. The night vision scope registered no human heat within its range, but he thought he was facing an adversary intelligent enough to be using shields or a distortion pulse.

He continued one block over to Winslow, still trying to amble along in the guise of a slightly overweight tourist—particularly overweight because of the arsenal of weaponry strapped to his body.

Winslow Street is a steep hill. The guard fence and the forest surrounding the monument are on the right as you ascend. On the left are some charmingly bohemian old houses—screenless windows open to reveal an antique lamp in a Tiffany shade, a faux-French street sign: *Rue de Winslow.* At the crest of the hill, also to the left, sits the squat brick silhouette of Provincetown High School—the enormous clock in its forehead stuck at 2:55. And there on the right, rising 252 feet and 7-1/2 inches from the ground, towering over all of Provincetown: the monument, a great granite arm reaching for the moon. The night sky still retained a deep dark blue, and the stone tower with its gargoyles and its columnated headpiece stood in vivid contrast against it. This night the tower appeared tilted, leaning slightly towards Clancy in a manner that felt both sinister and beckoning. If the devil was a building, he thought, it would look like this.

Cement steps led up to the main entrance which was, of course, locked.

According to plan, two policemen were up in the tower and two were patrolling the grounds.

Even with his nightscope, Clancy couldn't spot any cops on the ground, and he figured they were either skillful or dead.

The visitor's sign announced that there was no elevator to the top of the tower: just 60 ramps and 116 steps.

He knew it would be hot in there, and dark—just a few low-wattage ghost lights on each of the 60 floors…and what if the assailant had access to the master power and could plunge all 252 feet and 7-1/2 inches of it into instant blackness?

Then the nightscope.

But the scope couldn't see through granite. Couldn't see through the floor above.

Clancy jogged past the main entrance towards the darkness of High Pole Street.

The fence was lower in front of the industrial garbage bin; it was no longer barbed, and, by pre-arrangement, the police had left a small black emergency ladder leaning against it.

Though he was a middle-aged man, Clancy moved lightly and adroitly up the ladder. His heart was hammering, but his hands and feet still moved with agility.

He was proud of his tradecraft; and hell, he'd *written* this scene enough times.

"The Eagle has landed," he quietly and a little self-consciously spoke into his walkie-talkie. *The nearly-bald eagle….*

The flood lamps which lit the enormous tower cast enough light to make out a service trail cut through the trees.

There was a noise behind him.

He turned to see a flash of yellow shirt; he heard the snap of a twig, and the black police ladder disappeared.

Good, he thought. Everything by the book. Make it harder and noisier for the assailant to penetrate the perimeter, if he wasn't inside already. This assumed that the assailant was a *he*. Maybe it was Ann Coulter in her little black cocktail dress: "Tom, I don't want to kill you. I just want to squeeze your testicles in this nut cracker."

Cool.

Moving through the trees he could see that what looked like a large iron fire door had been pulled over the entrance to the tower. Welded to the iron door was a hasp for a padlock—but there was no padlock in place. The iron fire door was ajar—open about two inches to the darkness inside.

Clancy hoped the police hadn't removed the lock. Elementary tradecraft would have dictated your man on the outside replace the lock with a Myerwood balsa dummy. This way a quick visual inspection wouldn't arouse suspicion, but your operative could break the thing with one good push if he had to escape.

Didn't these guys read?

No, they were too busy preparing for Drag Bingo.

He'd write a special series of novels for Provincetown: *Tom Clancy's Homoland Security.*

"This is TomCat. Did you guys open the lock?"

No response. The night birds. The shimmering trill of 5,000 crickets.

"This is TomCat. Do you copy?"

No response.

The crickets were saying to him: ...*die, die, you're going to die...*

This is the night, the night you die....

Like hell it was. There was no way he was dying before he finished *Thirty Seconds Over Bethlehem*. The Pope would be asking him to speak at the Vatican when *that* one came out. He'd do the first reading at the papal summit at St. Peter's. *I'd like to dedicate this reading to my agent, Sol Schlesinger, and to Jesus Christ: two Jews I really admire.*

"This is TomCat. Did you guys pull the lock? Answer me?"

"All clear," answered the walkie-talkie.

Finish the job, Clancy, he told himself. Get this over with once and for all. Kill the crazy fucker before he nails another novelist. *You've got four cops and a coat full of weapons.*

He felt in his right-hand pocket. His fingers touched the barrel of a completely illegal weapon for a civilian to possess: the CIA-developed custom Lombard subminiature pistol with full-sized scope. It had been modeled on MI5's famously discontinued Odyssey series—a weapon which had been specifically designed for assassinations, though no one could admit this publicly. The Lombard was even smaller, lighter, with a wickedly accurate Zeiss optical scope tricked out with digital tracking that would automatically coordinate the trajectory of the barrel against the distance from the target, the movement of the target, and the movement of the gun itself. If your hand was steady enough for the 20th of a second it took to lock the scope and depress the firing pin, you *had* your target. There was no guesswork and no chance of missing unless your target was moving faster than light.

Would he have the 5.5 seconds he needed to pull the Lombard from his pocket, then attach and calibrate the scope?

Fuck the 5.5 seconds.

He didn't like walking into a dark building with an illegal, *classified* weapon drawn and fully armed—but, what the hell, he'd need more than his Liberian blood knife against this son of a bitch.

"TomCat. Inside the nest," he told the walkie-talkie.

No response.

All four cops are dead already, he thought.

He was inside.

He could feel a rug under his feet. Then stone.

Then the smell of stone.

Enough light from a single 15-watt bulb to see the dark maw opening to the left...the stairs leading up sixty floors. Sixty ramps. One hundred and sixteen steps.

"TomCat ascending."

No response. Then—startling in the dark—he heard: "All clear."

He attached the walkie-talkie to his belt.

He held the Lombard in his right hand and the Liberian blood knife, that nickel-plated corkscrew, in his left.

I'm fucking ready to kill somebody.

By the seventh floor he felt winded. The ramps were steeper than he'd imagined, and the effort to mount the stairs was growing increasingly more difficult.

Somewhere around the 16th floor he could hear music. He thought he must be dreaming, but by the 22nd floor he knew it was getting louder. Violin music, repeating itself, like some demented children's round. It was definitely coming from above.

"This is TomCat. What's the source of the music? Over."

"All clear."

What the fuck is this "all clear"?

He was asking a question about music, and the response was "all clear"?

Then he thought: Assailant has digitally recorded the cop saying "all clear." The cop was actually lying in a corner somewhere with his throat slit—or thrown overboard. But where could you throw anyone? There were no visible doors and the few narrow upright slits of windows cut into the stone weren't wider than Clancy's hand, and they were barred on the inside to keep the kids from dropping their Snapple bottles down 252 feet for the pleasure of hearing them smash on top of their parents' heads.

You could see the floodlights through the narrow windows—get a brief breath of the night air. The floodlights also revealed the webwork of cracks all through the stonework: ancient dust and filaments of hard halogen light. It was like that Hitchcock movie with the spider web of light on the staircase. And Clancy would end up like that female agent at the beginning of *The 39 Steps*, falling on Robert Donat's kitchen table with a steak knife sticking out from her clavicle. *"Deez men vill stop at nuhthink. You must egt qviglee! …egt qviglee…egt qviglee…."*

Suddenly he knew what the music was.

It was a recording of Bernard Herrmann's title music for *Vertigo*.

Oh, very funny, you cocksucker.

Of course.

Climbing up the steps of the old Spanish church.

Somebody ends up going off the roof, but he could no longer remember who.

At least this was a killer with a sense of humor.

Clancy was moving faster now. He was angry; he was determined.

The temperature was getting hotter. The stone walls, leaking their cracks of light, smelled older, more rotten, more malevolent.

The music was louder. It must have been a CD set on repeat, he thought. Or else the entire Universal Studios orchestra was on the roof. At union scale. On weekend rates. Christ, his death was going to cost this guy 100 grand.

A noise.

The floor upstairs.

Running upwards.

Clancy activated the Lombard scope. **CENTER TARGET** it read in ghostly blue letters along the bottom of the eyepiece.

"Somebody running. About 50th floor," he reported.

No response.

"Is it suspect?" he asked.

No response.

You're alone, Clancy.

Why is this guy running? Something's gone wrong. Guy realizes there's a police presence inside and out.

And nowhere to hide in this place. No service doors. No elevators. No restrooms. Just prison stone.

Deal with him, thought Clancy. Deal with him now or forever be running.

The guy got Grafton. The guy got Steel and Sittenfeld.

This was the end of the line.

The guy was up against Tom Fucking Clancy.

Noise again.

Running—Clancy turned the curve of the stairs and *saw*, actually saw a leg disappearing around the next set of stairs.

Clancy was running after him now.

"Target in sight."

Chase him right into the arms of the two cops on the roof.

Colder air.

There was a heavily barred observation hallway on the 58th floor—and the bars were sealed behind thick plastic so scratched you could barely see through it.

At the end of the observation hallway a plywood door

was swinging open. The lock had been torn away. *No admittance* was painted on the door.

These were the final stairs, and this, clearly, was the source of the music.

There was no light at all.

He attached the night-vision scope to his eyes like a pair of futuristic sunglasses. The scope registered nothing.

He moved up the last ramp and he was standing on top of Pilgrim Monument. There were no bars here, no plastic windows, just a stone patio about forty feet square surrounded by four stone columns holding the crown of the roof. The columns rose about thirty feet in the air. The wind was blowing fiercely. There was nothing to hold onto.

Across the roof, on the ground, sat what appeared to be a CD boom box. Clancy could see its red LED pilot light. And it played, again and again, the main theme from *Vertigo*.

Something in the corner caught his eye. A body. Yellow shirt. There were two bodies: both Provincetown cops. He couldn't tell if they were dead or drugged. A thin line of blood appeared to be spreading down both their necks from behind their ears.

"Man down!" he barked into the walkie-talkie. "Two men down! Roof!"

Movement startled him and he dropped the walkie-talkie. It fell to the hard stone; the case instantly broke and the battery went sailing.

He turned to see the most startling sight of his life. It appeared to be himself—dressed almost identically: the same red nylon windbreaker, the same ball cap, the same night-vision goggles. The figure was looking out at Provincetown.

Clancy, the real one, pulled his goggles off to see more clearly.

"What the—"

The figure in red by the window took a step towards the open air as if he might jump.

"No!" yelled Clancy.

The figure in red moved his other foot toward the edge.

The music repeated.

The wind was whipping his nylon windbreaker.

"Stop!' shouted Clancy.

The figure stood right on the edge when *another* pair of hands suddenly emerged from the darkness and pushed the figure out the window.

Oh, my God!

Clancy looked over the edge of the roof near him, and he heard for one horrible second the sound of the man in a windbreaker hurtling down like a broken kite.

He turned away from the window.

There was a pair of hands coming towards him. It was a man in a black suit, white shirt. Paper-white hair.

He recognized the man coming towards him, but he couldn't believe it.

It was Steve Martin.

Clancy raised the Lombard and fired wildly.

The last thing he saw were Martin's outstretched hands running towards him.

The last thing he heard was Martin's lunatic laughter:

"Her-her-her-HER-her!"

SIX

A SORT OF MIRACLE

Stephen King was scared. Leaving the iron gates of 47 West Broadway in Bangor had been difficult enough—Farewell, iron bats! Farewell, iron cobwebs!—but his general level of anxiety further increased when the radio cheerfully chirped that "legendary high-tech suspense writer" Tom Clancy had, apparently, leaped off the top of Pilgrim Monument in Provincetown, Massachusetts, the previous night. Clancy, the radio said, had gone to the police earlier that afternoon. The police had staked out both the area around and inside the monument. The officers later claimed they were waylaid and drugged by Clancy himself. When the officers awoke they found Clancy's body, hopelessly smashed, half-impaled on the decorative railing at the base of the monument. Clancy is survived by his former wife Wanda and his....

King turned up the radio of his black Cadillac hearse, but the bright-toned female d.j. at WKIT-FM had already moved on to local news.

King had actually felt a pang in his heart, a visceral throb of sympathetic anguish when he heard the part about "half-impaled on the decorative railing."

But the real horror was that his engine light was glowing a terrifying red, and the radiator gauge was moving rapidly towards H. The light had come on somewhere near Ellsworth; King was traveling south down 1A. It was after five and the daylight was beginning to fail. All he could think was: *Where am I going to find a mechanic at this hour?*

And what if the car just died?

Whom could he call?

Tabitha was God-knows-where—Swan's Island, he hoped, but this was pure conjecture.

"And, Mr. King," asked the Jack Webb-like policeman in his mind, "were you and your wife having any difficulties before she disappeared?"

He sighed. "Have you got a couple hours?"

"Just the facts, Mr. King."

He remembered a pinball machine from his youth: a detective in a thin tie looking at a woman wearing only a bath towel. "Just the facts, ma'am. Just the *bare* facts." That he still remembered this 50 years after he saw it was pretty alarming. *Maybe we're perpetually 10 years old,* he thought. Or *I'm* perpetually 10 years old.... Up in his room with his record player that could still play 78 r.p.m. records. His old 78 of Jerry Lewis performing "The Noisy Eater" with Lewis repeating the record's catchphrase in his terrible nasal cackle: *Oh, well, no matter.*

Where was he going to rent a car on a Saturday night in rural Maine? Or find a taxi willing to drive out to Bass Harbor? *This,* he thought, is true horror. Forget all the cinematic bullshit about haunted amulets and gypsy curses and ancient demons trapped down abandoned mineshafts— *this* was real horror: stuck in small-town America with no car, no friends, no family that gave a shit, and no means to get home. He honestly couldn't think of a single person to come get him.

Oh, well, no matter.

Christ, it had been a mistake to leave the house. He wasn't equipped for the world anymore...it felt as if he were driving in slow motion through the road company of *Freaks.* Everywhere he looked, the world seemed distorted: the

Asian men he had passed leaving Bangor—each twin dressed exactly alike in the same red shirt with the same-looking cell phone jammed to their ears. The storefronts were too bright, filled with photographs of models who looked like no one on the face of the earth. *This is what the world looks like when you've been alone too long.* The toothless, overweight women (sisters?) on the side of the road selling Maine blueberries— $3.00 a pint. The International House of E-Coli. A pest removal place with a huge, hideous plaster-of-Paris insect on its roof. He pronounced the word *exterminators* out loud and it actually made him feel sick. He passed a supermarket for medical supplies: King Kolon.

The temperature gauge was all the way over to the right, and he knew he had to pull over—park in the off-ramp to this freakshow.

A sign read Dedham, and he pulled the Cadillac into the wide gravel driveway of what a faded sign told him was once a horse farm and a dog kennel. It didn't seem to be much of anything now—except overgrown.

He turned off the motor. Even with the key removed, the electrical system made an unpleasant clicking noise—a buzzing relay.

He had written this scene one hundred times. *The roof was punched in on the right side giving it that slightly sinister look of all places that have been abandoned for a long time....* And the couple inside, he thought: amiable slackers who we find out are Satan's roadies. Satan will turn on them later in the novel when he grows tired of their timidity. He'll make the guy's testicles swell to the size of helium balloons; he'll make the girl's breasts become so massive she has to support them in bushel baskets. Then the bitter couple will be banned forever from Hell. Forced to walk the earth painfully eking out a living as a derelict traveling magic act: Cups and Balls.

King shook his head. He was becoming dangerously unbalanced.

The house he'd pulled in front of was a one-storey farmhouse covered in rust-colored shingles. The front door was open, and he shouted into the screen: "Hello! Anybody there?"

There was a black Jetta parked in the driveway, and he walked around towards the back. At the side door, also open, he called: "Hello! Hello!"

In the backyard stood some abandoned kennel-cages, although he could hear a dog barking somewhere. There were overgrown vegetable gardens and a barn. From the barn emerged a couple in their twenties. They were amiable slackers. She was a big-boned young woman in a tube top and jeans. There was a tattoo on her shoulder of a man's body with a devil's head. She had a completely round face and short ash-blonde hair. The guy was much thinner: unshaved, dark hair and eyes. He held a beer can.

"Hey, I'm terribly sorry to bother you," began King. "My car overheated."

"Dude, you drive a hearse?"

"There's nobody dead inside. Not that I know of, in any case."

"Who are The Prisoners?"

"I think the car used to belong to a band."

"Cool."

The girl whispered something. Then she spoke aloud. "You're Stephen King, aren't you?"

"Yes, I am."

"I told you," she said. "We just watched that show on TV. Stephen King's Stories of Mystery and Imagination."

"Dreamscapes and Nightmares."

"Right."

"Yeah," added the guy. "That was fucked up."

"Did you like it?"

They looked at each other.

"Yeah, well we only saw the first couple of 'em," said the girl.

"Did you hate it?"

"No," she said. "We didn't hate it."

"But you stopped watching?"

The guy was studying the car.

"Tell me. Really. What did you think? I'd like to know," said King.

"CGI," said the guy, still studying the car.

"What?"

"Computer generated imagery. Too much CGI. It's, like, the whole series was special effects." He scratched his stubble. "I don't know anything about television."

A passing driver honked.

"He's honking at me," said the girl.

"But I thought the show was too special-effects heavy," said the guy. "The episodes seemed like an excuse for Industrial Light and Magic to show us another cat with no eyes, another toy soldier come to life, another underground serpent crashing out of the pavement. Dude, that stuff just has no *weight* anymore, you know? When you can do *anything,* when the walls can turn to blood, and the water can come straight up out of the bathtub, it doesn't feel even remotely scary. It's like watching a *drawing* or something. Nothing's at stake. We've got these two-dimensional characters who don't even speak or act like human beings— and they come face to face with these monsters who don't even feel *remotely* threatening. Dude, as an audience member, there's no one to *empathize* with, you know? No sympathetic characters we care about. I mean, dude, it's like the difference between Hideo Nakata's original Japanese *Ringu*, which is, like, all subtlety and suggestion and this disturbingly Freudian subtext, and then you compare it to Gore Verbinski's *The Ring*—you know, the American remake? Which is, like, this cartoonish shitpile with an unappealing mother and equally unlikable son up against this tidal wave of computer-generated blood. I mean, dude, you can enjoy it as some sort of vaguely fucked-up Wes Craven gorefest, but you just don't *care*. And the whole ethical *core* of the original, which is, like, *Who would you kill to save yourself?*—and, man, that is a *powerful* question—that's all lost. In the remake, man, the entire moral *nucleus* of the original is dissolved into this cloyingly saccharine DreamWorks-sentimental-spectacle that isn't even *marginally* affecting. You know? Pump up the John Williams music until the audience is deluded into believing they're actually *feeling* something. I mean, dude, go back to something like Shirley Jackson's *The Haunting*, and what is it? It's about absolutely nothing at all. It's all *suggestion*, man: the creak on the stairs, the shadow on the wall, and Christ, you're on the edge of your seat. And what's *Rebecca* about? Really? It's about nothing at all. It's all suggestion, man. That's what's scary. Nothing at all and your heart is pounding. And then you compare that to *Stephen King's Dreamscapes and Nightmares* and, nothing personal, man, but the TV show's a fucking joke. But, like I said, you don't have to listen to me. I don't know anything about television. I'm unemployed, man."

"Right," said King quietly.

"Do you have a rag? I'll check the radiator. And I can fill you up with some water from the hose; maybe we can get you to a gas station."

"There aren't any gas stations open now," said the girl.

The tow truck guy from AAA couldn't get the hearse started. "I can give you a jump. Or I can fix a flat," the guy said. "But I can't help you with this. You can hear the battery's good. She just won't turn over."

"What can you do?"

"I can tow you three miles for free, and then it's three dollars per mile."

"I think it's the solenoid, man," said the bearded guy. "The solenoid or the thermostat. Put it on *heat*. I know that sounds crazy. But sometimes it opens the thermostat if it's stuck."

Three telephones didn't stop ringing at the Keller Salvage Yard in Dedham where King found himself marooned with Mike, the owner and operator.

Night was coming on.

His car was dead. There were no cabs in Dedham. There were no rent-a-car agencies still open in the middle of Maine on a Saturday night. The phone at the Enterprise car rental office in Bangor simply rang unanswered, and when he called the national number they told him it wouldn't open till Monday at nine.

King thought that if there was a motion-picture camera in his head (and he often thought there was), then it was rising now in a crane shot—leaving him slumped despairingly in this torn black office chair, sitting at this small round kitchen table next to this vending machine filled with sad-looking pretzels that smelled as if they'd been soaked in transmission fluid. An oil slick on the cement floor. Decals on the window: *24 Hr. Towing AAA. Auto & Truck Repairs. Official Station. Monday-Friday 9 a.m. to 5 p.m. Saturday 10 a.m.-1 p.m.* Three phones ringing: one on the desk and two cell phones.

"Jesus Christ," said Keller. "They don't stop. Keller's Salvage...okay...tell 'em we're coming, but we're going to be about 40 minutes, Pete's doing the flat in West Franklin." The other cell phone. "Holy Christ." He checked the second number. "Scott, where the hell are you?" He turned to King. "Look, I'll take a look at your car when things quiet down a little. Just give me a couple of minutes. My other son's supposed to be here. But he races on Saturday. I've been working straight through since this morning. I missed lunch and dinner."

"You want some pretzels?" asked King. "Take some pretzels."

"Here, I'll show you what I do with them."

Keller carried a pretzel to the back of the office where he tried feeding it to an iguana in a tall green cage. "Come on, Gory. Get that out of your water and eat it."

One desk was white. The one jammed next to it with the computer was black. Filing cabinets—also black. Footprints of oil and grease led back to the bathroom. An Indian blanket over the service window kept the customers' prying eyes out of the shop. A corkboard pegged with car keys. Keller smelling of body odor and 40-weight motor oil.

If our crane shot pulled back further, thought King, we'd see his poor wounded hearse, towed directly in front of the office. A red and white sign read *No Parking Anytime.* The siding had been removed where an old garage entrance used to be. It was nailed shut with six large sheets of plywood—a support rafter sticking out of the front of the plywood like the plank of a ship. Two tires leaned against each other. A six-foot piece of fiberboard on its side, a broken wooden pole, a gas-powered compressor amid a litter of black hoses, a small dirty white dog lying on the stones and cigarette butts, leashed to the air compressor in front of an industrial trash bin....

King closed his eyes. He felt hot and hopeless. And still the phones rang. "We can get him, but it's going to be at least 50 minutes...fax it over."

This is horror, he thought. Friendless on a Saturday night in Dedham, Maine. No car. No cell phone. No one to call if you *had* a cell phone...and the woman whom you've shared your life with...gone...probably *relieved* to be out of your presence, playing her own music, no more John Fogerty singing about centerfield. No more of her husband's neuroses and his stupid, pathetic pettiness and his suffocating routine.

He said aloud, "Tabby, save me."

"Don't look good," said Keller. He dipped a blackened finger into the open radiator—then examined the finger with the cool detachment of a man who had been fooling around with motors for sixty years. "Oil. You see that on top? And look in the overflow. You've got some kind of sludge in there."

"What does that mean?"

"Well, you don't want to have oil in the cooling system. You're leaking oil. Which probably means you've blown the head gasket."

"I pulled over when it was running hot."

"How long were you running it hot?"

"Just a couple of minutes."

"A couple of minutes is all it takes. You see, the engine is made of two different metals and they expand at different rates when they're hot. They pull apart." He indicated with his dark hands. "And you've breached the gasket."

"Is it something you can repair?"

"No, no, no. This is a *huge* job. Basically, you've got to pull the entire motor apart."

"Are you kidding me?"

"You're talking about a two-week job. Minimally. I'll have to tow you on Monday over to the GM place in Ellsworth."

"Are you serious? What do I do till Monday? The rental places are all closed."

Nightmare in Dedham, King thought.

Good concept but too much CGI.

"Where are you headed?"

"Swan's Island."

"What the hell you want to go there for?"

"My wife's there."

"Then why doesn't *she* come get you?"

"She doesn't know I'm here. We're separated."

Keller thought for a second. The phone was ringing inside the office. "Ferry doesn't run this late anyway."

"Can I get to Bass Harbor? I think I can find a place to stay if I can get there."

"You ever been to Bass Harbor? It's a dump. A fishing wharf, a pizza joint, a place that sells model rockets, and a lot of weeds. There's no hotels there."

"Is there any way I can get there tonight? I'm sure I can find someplace. Somebody'll rent me a room."

"Why do you need to get there tonight?"

"Look. If my wife took the ferry, then she may have

left her car there. And I've got a set of keys for her car. I've got to find her, okay? Just take my word for it."

Keller scratched his face. His cell phone rang. He checked the incoming number. "Pete, did you get the Franklin flat? Look, Pete, you want to earn a little money? I've got Stephen King here. The writer. Yeah. He needs to get to Bass Harbor tonight. Right. On Mount Desert Island. Way down at the bottom. I figure it's going to be at least an hour and a half each way. Are you interested? We figure…" Keller looked at King. "A buck and a quarter?"

King nodded. Thank God he had some cash. Plus a little more to tip the guy.

"Right. Bass Harbor. Okay." He turned to King. "He thinks he can do it. He's got to call his wife first and make sure she doesn't need him. He can be here in about twenty minutes."

The phone rang again in the office.

"Jesus Christ!" said Keller.

King sat in the beat-up black office chair and filled out all the information needed for the towing on Monday— including his VISA number and his unlisted home phone number. He couldn't believe he was giving this information out to some salvage yard in Dedham. By Monday he figured everybody in Keller's family would be driving brand-new hybrids with their trunks full of high-definition televisions.

The guy's a millionaire, Dad. He doesn't care.

The twenty minutes turned into an hour and fifteen.

In a moment of despair, King called Tabitha's cell phone. His hands were shaking. There was no answer, but he heard her voice: *I'm not available right now. Please leave a message.*

He was unable to speak.

***

Dedham to Ellsworth to Trenton.

An airport with an old biplane offered rides to tourists. The inevitable Wal-Mart.

The Trenton lobster pound was open, and King insisted Pete stop. King ordered two lobster rolls. The air smelled richly of wood smoke as six outdoor brick fireplaces churned six iron kettles of boiling water, and the lobsters, in their carrying nets, cracked and sizzled inside them. King suddenly felt like asking for a job. Maybe he could spend the rest of this life shuttling lobsters out to the fireplaces. Haul wood. Tend the fires. Never read another book; another dismissive review. Talk to the tourists about where they'd come from.

If Tabby was here he'd have asked the lady in the green sundress for a cup of ice cubes. Tabby liked to suck on ice. She put ice in her white wine. She couldn't ride in the backseat of a car; it made her nauseous. She was forever putting down the sun visor to check her reflection in the illuminated mirror.

How did that old Sinatra song go? *Things I found hard to praise/Right now would seem sublime.*

Pete, the driver of the pick-up truck in which they were traveling, was in his late thirties. Thin red hair. He was, thought King, a sort of hopelessly good-natured Li'l Abner type: sweet, responsible, mercilessly exploited by people around him who knew he just couldn't say no. He ate his lobster roll as they crossed the bridge over to Mount Desert Island—which Pete correctly pronounced as "dessert." "Don't usually eat lobstuh," he said. "Too expensive." Each lobster roll was thirteen dollars, and King was happy to pay it. Pete told stories about his mother: "She's 81. I take her shopping every Sunday mawning. And then we go the flea mahkuts. And *that's* three or four owwuhs. She has to go through every goshdarn item."

"You're a good son. How's the lobster roll?"

"Delicious. And then my sistuh-in-law didn't want her dog anymaw. It's this cute little Irish collie I think is the kind, so she wanted me to give it to the pet staw; well, she *knew* I wasn't going to do that. So now *I've* got the goshdarn thing. I almost stepped on it this mawning." He laughed, took another bite of the roll. "It likes to sleep in the laundry room, you know? Unduh all the sheets. Well, I didn't even *see* her this mawning. Almost stepped right on 'er. She sleeps in my bed. Goes right unduh the covuhs. All the way unduh. I keep thinking she's gonna suffocate down theyuh. I keep checking that she's still breathing."

Somesville to the right, down 102, past the guy with a lawn full of old washboards, license plates, glass bottles, broken lobster traps, pith helmets, tool boxes, fishing sinkers, buoys, cane chairs, military boots, and a Zenith Wavemagnet shortwave radio that had sat outside for twelve winters.

Campwood for sale. Two dollars a bundle.

A dentist.

Instead of *No Vacancy* a wooden sign read *Sorry*.

"What *is* that?" asked King. He pointed to a little plastic figure hanging down from the rearview mirror. It was a man's body with a devil's head. "I've seen that before."

"That's Gory," said Pete. "It's supposed to wahd off evil."

"It looks pretty evil." King examined the plastic man.

"Gory the Mute."

"What's that?"

"I don't think it's anything really. It's, you know, like Big Foot or Sasquatch or somethin'. It's s'posed to live on the islands out heah. On Little Cranberry, I think. Or Swan's."

"I never heard of this."

"I've huhd it my whole life. My friend Bobby in Bass Hahbah? He raises partridges theyuh? He says it kills his buhds at night. Finds them with the blood sucked out of 'em."

"Do you believe that?"

"I tell him it's probably a bayuh. Or a wolf."

"Wolves drink blood?"

"I don't know. Where are you staying in Bass Hahbah?"

"I just have to take the ferry to Swan's Island. God, I am suddenly so tired."

"The ferry won't run till nine tomorrah. I don't know if it even runs at *all* on Sundays. I can call Bobby. He might be able to put you up for the night. If you don't mind the partridges."

"The partridges don't bother me," said King still examining the plastic figurine. "It's Gory the Mute I'm a little uncomfortable with."

Small non-reflective black and white signs began appearing on the side of 102A: *Swan's Island Ferry.*

Manset. Seawall.

There was a cold dry breeze coming from the west off Blue Hill Bay. The houses were getting more thinly spaced. The streetlights were fewer in number. Broad fields of scrub grass looked gray under the moonlight. Then the sudden sharp smell of fishing bait—and a dozen cars parked on a sandy lot near the water.

King could hear the water lapping against the stony shore. It *sounded* cold. Unforgiving.

Then he saw it.

"Hold it, Pete."

King climbed down from the cab. About five cars in from the ferryboat house stood his wife's black BMW.

She was here.

She stood on this ground.

He tried his spare key. It turned. The car smelled like her. He started the engine, and both the air conditioner and the CD player came on. *Essential difference between a man and woman,* he thought. Women leave on the accessories; men don't. It was one of those absurd gender-specific issues—like the lint filter on the drier. Men scraped it clean after drying a single sock. Women ran it until you could knit a sweater from the two-inch wad of accumulated lint.

That's why you love her, Stephen.

The CD was the live Laura Nyro Fillmore concert from 1971; it was a concert that Tabitha had traveled to New York to attend—"completely stoned," she'd confessed to him. Tabby the bad seed. He had a hundred names for her lively temper: Hothead Joe. Full Ruff. Full Display.

An Alibris bookmark on the front seat. In her handwriting was written a phone number on Swan's Island: the last cell-phone call she'd made.

Of course, her phone probably wouldn't work on the island. That's why there was no answer when he'd called from Keller's.

He locked the car. There was a parking ticket on the windshield. He'd check the date later.

"Everything all right?" asked Pete. The truck was still running, headlights cutting the mothy, crickety night.

"One minute," said King.

He walked to the ferry house which was locked. The ferry was apparently moored somewhere else for the night.

There was a yellow bug light on the frame of the house, and it illuminated a faded schedule: five ferries per day in the winter; six in the summer. A water-stained warning to tourists: Swan's Island has no restaurants, no liquor stores, no public restrooms, no recreational facilities, no shopping area, no public hiking trails, no public bicycle trails, and no public beaches.

Welcoming, King thought.

Another sign announced that the ferry, the Captain Henry Lee, took approximately 30 minutes to reach the island.

Someone was approaching, descending down the gentle, stony hill. It was a middle-aged man in a blue shirt, blue jeans with suspenders, a big-brimmed sunhat and a walking stick with a leather safety strap.

In his head he heard Tabby's voice peg the guy: Ragtime Cowboy Joe.

And he knew, at that moment, that he was going to hear Tabby's voice in his head for the rest of his life. He was going to hear the private code they spoke. It was like the secret message they gave each other in their first editions. He'd sign the first copy for her: *With all the love in my heart, Stephen*—and then, starting on page 23 (he'd been 23 when they started this game) he'd place a dot under a printed letter. He'd continue the message on every third page. His message was always the same: I-L-O-V-E-Y-O-U.

There was shuffling in the grass behind Ragtime Cowboy Joe and four speckled-brown stout-looking birds followed in his wake.

"Stephen King?"

"Yes."

"I'm Bobby. Bobby Whyte." He extended his hand.

As if on cue, a bird from the reedy grass loudly whistled: *bob-bobwhite!* It was so loud and so clearly enunciated it was comical.

"Quiet, Hoppy!" he said. "I live just up there." He pointed to a tiny cottage that looked as if it might have belonged in a French village. "You can rest a bit until we can find somebody to take you over to the island."

"Do you have a boat?"

"Yes," said Bobby. "But I don't go out there anymore."

"Why not?"

He shrugged. He poked his walking stick into the loose ground. "People don't seem to come back from Swan's Island."

Bob-bobwhite! sang the bird in loud agreement.

"Deek! Hoppy! Quiet!"

"You're telling me people are being abducted?"

"I don't know what I'm telling you," said Bobby, and he threw some corn to the partridges. "You know that guy Ken Lay? The guy from Enron?"

"He died last summer, didn't he?"

Bobby nodded, looked down at the holes he was imprinting in the ground. "Can I tell you something? I swear to God I saw Ken Lay getting on that ferry yesterday morning at 7:30."

A *ching* from a thumb-operated bell, and another figure rode up on a child's bike.

"My brother Robby," said Bobby.

In a stroke that delighted King's love of the absurd, the brothers were identical twins. Each wore suspenders and jeans. Each wore a broad-brimmed sunhat. Robby wore a blue seersucker shirt and eyeglasses. In the basket of his bike was a covey of bobwhites that appeared extremely comfortable being driven around.

"This is Stephen King," said Bobby.

"Man, I loved the *Dark Tower*," said Robby. "I read all six."

"Thank you," said King and shook his hand, which was larger and colder than he imagined.

"So when can we expect *The Even Darker Tower*?"

"Soon!" said King.

"I got mine pre-ordered on Amazon!" said Robby.

"Terrific."

The Whytes lived in a tiny shingled cottage with a brick chimney next to the front door. The chimney was sealed at the top in an arch with a birdhouse-shaped opening to ventilate the smoke. Ivy grew halfway up the chimney. The French barn door at the front of the cottage was braced open—no screen door—and the many bobwhites about the place moved in and out at will. In the weeds sat a small abandoned-looking truck that read *POISON* in faded red letters on the tank.

The cottage was a converted stable. Rough wooden planks painted white: still dark at the knotholes and the seams. Exposed ceiling beams also painted white. There was one large-sized bed under the slanting ceiling and another small one by the tiny bathroom. The two side windows were braced open with pieces of driftwood.

King sat at the kitchen table.

The brothers sat at the couch.

A kerosene lamp that had been converted to electricity hung over the kitchen table, and its dim bug-speckled bulb cast the only illumination in the room.

A dog's bowl filled with corn sat on the floor near the kitchen sink, and the bobwhites pecked at it.

"You guys make a living raising birds?" asked King, who gratefully sipped the Geary's ale they offered him.

From the yard came a loud whistle: *bob-bobwhite!*

Bobby (blue-shirt, no glasses) tilted back his head:

"Just listen to the bobwhite!"

Robby (seersucker, glasses) immediately added:

"He never could sing right."

And suddenly they were half-singing:

"You should hip him to the latest sound/And the talk that's going 'round."

"Well, I was talking to the parakeet/And he said, 'Man, now about that beat.'"

"How *about* that beat?"

"Hey, bobwhite! Ain't you gonna swing tonight?"

"Several people heard the albatross..."

"Yes?"

"Whisper, 'Robert is on the sauce!'"

"I know for a fact he's on the wagon."

"Bobwhite! Nothing but a neophyte."

"Bob, what's that word mean?"

"Amateur!"

They both cracked up laughing like little kids, though they were both clearly in their 40s, and they slapped the couch in joyful silliness. "We love that old Johnny Mercer/Bobby Darin record," explained Bobby (blue shirt). "That's all we ever listen to. We know the whole damn thing."

"Sounds like a train song if you ask me!" said Robby (seersucker); they were off into another acapella shtick.

"My cutey's due at 2:22/She's coming through on a DC-2."

"You've got a girl in space!"

"I met each Boeing jet/But she hasn't shown up yet."

"Try the airport!"

King watched in delighted disbelief. "If you guys can't make a living raising birds, you can always go on *American Idol*."

"More like *The Gong Show*."

"We don't make a living from the birds," said Bobby. "We sell some to hunters. They train their birddogs with them. Some people eat them."

"It's quail," said Robby. He held a bobwhite lovingly in his hands. "But we wouldn't eat one."

"We raise 'em as pets."

"People buy these as pets?"

"No, they're *our* pets."

"We sell these lanyards, too." He handed King a lanyard printed with a parade of bobwhites.

"Take one. So you'll remember us."

"Believe me, I'll remember you." King hooked his car keys to the lanyard. "And your crazy birds."

"We make our money on other stuff."

"We're exterminators."

"Oh, right, I saw the truck."

"Yeah, you know: rats, roaches, nasty shit. We just won't kill any birds."

"No birds."

"And you guys get work?"

"Too much work. Out in the shed there, we got enough poison to kill everybody on Swan's Island."

"Which probably wouldn't be a bad thing," said Bobby.

"What's going on out there?" asked King.

The two brothers looked at each other.

From outside came: *bob-bobwhite!*

"Listen to the bobwhite," said Bobby.

"He could never sing right!" sang Robby.

The next morning King stood by the shore of Bass Harbor waiting for a private motorboat to take him to Swan's Island. At that sunny, empty hour the bobwhites were particularly active, and the grassy fields were loud with their whistles. *Bob-bobwhite!*

The Whyte brothers had let King sleep in their outdoor hammock under a tiny shingled shade-roof with mosquito netting (only partially effective) hanging down from the support posts. King couldn't sleep anyway. As Macbeth had so aptly said, his mind was full of scorpions. He was scared of Swan's Island; he was scared of what it might cost to repair his car; he was scared of the affable Whyte brothers who might just quietly exterminate *him* during the night and feed him to their carnivorous bobwhites. As the dawn approached he could read *Hatteras Hammocks* where the ropes converged.

The Whytes were too spooked to take him to Swan's Island, but they knew someone who would—a "scientist" they called him, though they couldn't actually explain what he researched. "Michael Liguori," said Robby.

"Everybody around here calls him Gnome."

His brother added: "He's always carrying around one of those aluminum briefcases."

Liguori had told the brothers he was happy to take King with him on his motorboat. King offered one hundred dollars for the trip, ("I'll pay you as soon as I can get to a machine.") but Liguori refused all payment: he was a naturalist; he was going to the island early in the morning anyway.

"How early?"

"Five-thirty?"

Liguori's motorboat—a small rowboat with an outboard—pulled up exactly on time.

King climbed down a metal ladder on the dock into the unsteady boat.

Liguori shook his hand warmly.

There, indeed, was his famous aluminum briefcase. Liguori was a tall man, about 6'3", broad shouldered, perhaps in his late 50s. His head was completely shaved and a small black mole on the back of his skull stood out so startlingly that King kept thinking there was a fly walking on his head. Liguori wore a thick dark moustache, khaki shorts with a phone clipped to the waist, a khaki shirt and sandals. There was something about him, King thought, evocative of the "good soldier": strong, earnest, unsubtle, even slightly dumb-looking, and capable, of course, of killing you without a second's hesitation if ordered to do so.

"It's an honor to m-m-meet you," said Liguori who navigated the boat by compass, as the island was not visible. "Robby tells me you're st-st-starting work on *The Even Darker Tower*."

His stammer was painful.

"That's what I told my publisher. I'll have to see what the reality is."

"I thought I read somewhere that you were r-r-retiring."

"That was my plan. But, you know, you wake up one morning, and there's a story lying next to you on the pillow. Then the story keeps getting more complicated. It's like some virus. And you feel if you don't get it out it's going to kill the host."

"Sounds like a k-k-kind of curse."

"Not a curse," said King. "Hardly that. More like a machine you can't shut off. You pull the plug, and it still keeps writing sentences. I read that Richard Rodgers once said that if he didn't compose music every day he got constipated. It's strange. It really is a *physical* thing. What do you do, Mr. Liguori?"

"Michael. I'm a scientist. I study theories of l-l-language."

"Like whether dolphins speak?"

"S-s-something like that."

"The Whyte brothers said people call you Gnome. I'm sitting here thinking why would they call a big guy like you Gnome?"

He shrugged and smiled. "Why do they call a guy with no hair C-C-Curly?" He turned towards the spray and the morning light and the choppy green-white of the water. "Sometimes you see seals out here." Then: "Can I ask you something, Mr. King? And you can tell me if this is n-n-none of my business, okay?"

King smiled and waited for: *Where do you get your ideas from?*—which was polite-speak for: How fucked up *are* you to write all that weird shit? Or: What kind of Blimpie-sized blunt did you smoke before you wrote *Cujo*?

Instead, quite refreshingly, the question was: "Tell me, Mr. Bachman, do you ever get tired of being Stephen King?"

King gave the dopey-looking guy (shaved head and mole which looked like a housefly) a serious reappraisal.

"Mr. Bachman...," said King softly.

It was a reference, of course, to that series of NAL paperbacks he'd published in the late seventies/early eighties under the name of Richard Bachman. They were drugstore books: lurid thrillers with that terrible 70's artwork! *RAGE— a novel by Richard Bachman.* A longhaired kid with a big belt buckle sitting on a teacher's desk. Legs of a dead body, female, skirt hiked up as high as drugstore sensibility would permit. And those ludicrously melodramatic loglines! "His Twisted Mind Turned a Quiet Classroom into a Dangerous World of Terror." Signet logo in the upper corner—1977 price: $1.50!

A dollar fifty was all it was worth, he thought: those psychologically overwrought stories he'd write over a blizzard weekend in a sort of airless fever-dream that he could hardly imagine now. *Like a virus.* If it doesn't get voiced it kills the host. There was *The Long Walk* (now $1.95!): "In a future America, the Marathon is the Ultimate Sports Competition—a Novel of Chilling, Macabre Possibility." The only really chilling element about the novel was the assumption that old lady Houlihan, standing in Bangor Drugs waiting for her laxatives, would know what the hell "macabre" meant. *Roadwork* ($2.65): "His Life was in the Path of the Wrecking Ball—But He Wouldn't Budge." And, weighing in at a whopping $2.50, and source material for a cinematic classic: *The Running Man*: "Welcome to America in 2035 When the Best Men Don't Run for President. They Run for their Lives."

By the time he'd written *Thinner*, Steven Brown, a writer and bookstore clerk, had figured out who Richard Bachman was, and the game was over.

"How many times can a writer reinvent himself?" asked Liguori. "How many times should he *need* to?"

King looked out at the water. "You seem to know a great deal about me."

"I told you: I'm interested in language. You asked about my nickname? It's not g-n-o-m-e. It's N-o-a-m."

"Ah. Like Noam Chomsky."

"My father, Alphonsus Liguori, Jr., studied with Chomsky at U.P-P-Penn. He and Chomsky did research together as Junior Fellows at Harvard. My father followed him back to MIT in 1955. They collaborated on a groundbreaking paper called 'Logical Structures of Linguistic Theory.'"

"Didn't Chomsky reinvent grammar around then?"

"Yes. *Syntactic Structures.* 1957. T-t-transformational grammar. Language studies have never been quite the same. He and my father were no longer s-s-speaking by then."

King chuckled. "Two linguists not speaking. That sounds like a book. A not very good book. Later adapted into a failed sitcom."

"I'm interested in writers. And the client I represent is even *more* interested."

"Who's your client?"

"A man who wants to make you an offer."

"And why doesn't this man make the offer himself?"

"He prefers to let others speak for him."

King turned towards Liguori. "Are you kidnapping me?"

"On the contrary. I'm taking you to see your w-w-wife."

Liguori gunned the motor.

The island was finally coming into view. There was a high cliff jutting from a luxuriant forest. It was a tableau in vivid primary colors: the deep greens of the hills, the choppy blue of the sea, a red kayak, the flapping of a white and blue awning on a cliffside home. Bright, sunny, welcoming.

"What do you think?" asked Liguori.

"It looks like the place they took Patrick McGoohan to."

"*That's* a p-p-pretty metaphor. The island has three small communities within it: Atlantic, Minturn, and

Swan's Island. Only about 200 year-round residents: fishermen, retirees; there's even a small p-p-printing press on the island."

"And where's this 'compound' you were speaking of?"

"The Compound is on the western side where there's no town, and there's no tourism. The land is privately owned."

"By your mysterious client."

"Among others."

"I'm having a hard time visualizing this."

Liguori steered the boat to the left, giving wide berth to the more populated parts of the island.

"My client has c-c-created the Compound as an escape."

"A place you can't leave?"

"Why would you want to leave, Mr. King? What's w-w-waiting for you back on shore? Another negative review for *Cell* in the *Sunday Times Book Review*?"

"Hey, the daily *Times* was mixed."

"…another bill…another obligation…another interview with another reporter who b-b-brings to the table all the sensitivity of…"

"…A Goddamn toilet seat?"

"One of S-S-Salinger's great lines, wasn't it?"

"Don't tell me Salinger's on the island?"

"I told you, I can't answer specific questions—it would defeat the whole p-p-purpose of the Compound. But what my client is offering you, Mr. King, is a kind of p-p-paradise. A refuge. What did Tennessee Williams write? *A cleft in the rock of the world that I could hide in*?"

"You're very well read for the bad guy."

"I'm *n-n-not* the bad guy."

"You're an envoy for the bad guy?"

Liguori smiled. "You want to know who the b-b-bad guy is? It's the mechanic in Dedham who's going to tell you on Monday morning that you've b-b-blown your head gasket, and that it's a two-thousand dollar repair. Two thousand if you're lucky. The bad guy is a world out there so t-t-treacherous and so filled with maniacs and thugs that you have to live in a house with bars on the windows and a $75,000 alarm system."

"A *hundred* and seventy-five thousand. And dare I ask how you know all this stuff about me?"

"Computers leave a long paper trail, Mr. King. So do credit cards. B-b-but I told you, I'm not the bad guy."

"Okay. I'll bite. *Who's* the bad guy?"

"The bad guy is the critic who tells you that your last book isn't nearly as good as your earlier ones. And then tells you that your *next* book lacked the 'outright passion' of the b-b-book she panned the previous month."

"Tell me about it."

"Just imagine. No more insurance to pay. No more apologies at the National Book Foundation's Medal for Distinguished Service to American Letters dinner for accepting an award that nobody f-f-fucking wanted to give you."

"Cocksuckers. First, they *give* you the award, then half of them head straight to their websites and whine that you didn't deserve it."

"Imagine instead a place where you can write if you *feel* like it—where you can *not* write—and nobody ever says: 'Whatever happened to Stephen King?' Where you can publish if you want. Of course, your novels will be 'lost' manuscripts or p-p-posthumous books. But, believe me, you can k-k-keep that racket going for quite a long time. Look at Truman C-C-Capote. Is there a year that goes by that we haven't discovered another 'lost early novel' by Capote?"

"Is Capote on the island?"

"I can't answer that while you're still in the r-r-realm of the living."

"Now *that* has a sinister ring to it."

Liguori gestured to the cliff: the white and blue awnings on the cliffside houses appeared as sharp and clear as newly-minted coins. "*This* looks sinister to you?"

"No," said King. He watched a flock of what might have been cranes lift from the shoreline in unison and turn against the bright blue sky like a pattern of iron filings suddenly aligned by a magnet. "It looks like something I've always imagined."

"Many great writers and artists have m-m-made the choice you're about to make."

"How many?"

Liguori held a finger to his lips.

"Wait a minute. These writers I've been reading about recently? The ones who have been mysteriously killed? You're telling me—"

Liguori again put his finger to his lips and shook his head—as if to say: *We can't talk about that.*

King thought back to what he'd read in the newspapers. Grafton disappearing down the "terrifying abyss" of Reichenbach Falls. Steel and Sittenfeld dissolving in a Jacuzzi full of sulphuric acid. Clancy's mangled body impaled on a railing; of course, it could have been *any* body, dressed as Clancy, and threaded with enough ID to make the identification all but certain.

"Look," said King. "You told me you're taking me to see my wife?"

"Very possibly."

"I can live without publishing; I can live without my public; I can even—God forgive me for saying this—live without my charming children. I'm honest enough to know that kids in their 30s don't give two shits about their parents except as a never-ending supply of money to bail out one more dog-ass marriage, one more dog-ass career decision. And when their parents die—hopefully soon—it means even *more* money. I accept that. That's what the promise of millions of dollars does to anybody. But what I most strenuously *don't* accept is never seeing Tabby again. I don't want to get sentimental on you, Mr. Liguori, but not seeing her ever again is the one thing I cannot accept. And, honestly, I would kill you if you've hurt her. Wouldn't think one second about it. I'd kill you if you tried to keep me from seeing her."

"You're not seeing her now."

"I have the *chance* to. I have the chance to win her back."

"I wouldn't have taken you as that r-r-romantic or that heroic."

"It would surprise you to know what an emotional guy I am."

"Then why don't you write about th-th-that guy?"

"Because," said King, and he felt an old anger rising inside him, "when readers shove 29 dollars down for a Stephen King hardback they want a story about a guy with knitting needles stuck in his eyes; they want half-dead corpses rising out of the bathtub; they want Satan running the returns register at Best Buy; they want dead cats hanging from the oak trees; they want a 200-page chase scene in which Everyman tries to run the fuck away from the Screaming Dead Thing. And they want it *over* and fucking *over* again."

"And what do you *want* to write about?"

"I don't particularly want to write about anything.

Sometimes I think I want to *erase* words. I want silence. Sometimes I think the world has too many words."

"So s-s-stop writing."

"And do *what*?" said King, and his voice was angry and even a little desperate. "Sit around on your luxury island all day and watch the birds and jerk off in my kayak?" He took a long breath. "Actually that doesn't sound half bad."

"And the big, ugly w-w-world out there? The world that's p-p-preordered *The Even Darker Tower*?"

"Oh, fuck the *Dark Tower*. I never liked that series anyway. It felt like carpentry, you know? Like making a chair. It was a well-made chair; I'm proud of my professional ability, you know? I deliver the goods. But it was a chair the world didn't need or even particularly want."

"We're here," said Liguori.

He pulled the boat into a small private pier on the far western side of the island.

Don't get out, thought King. *Knock this stammering fuck out, steal the boat, and get the fuck outta here.*

"Follow me," said Liguori warmly.

"The wine is local," said Steve Martin. He'd brought out two glasses on a silver tray. "You'll like it." In his elegant black summer suit and tie-less white shirt, Martin might have been a waiter at a Bar Harbor bed and breakfast. "I'm an enormous fan of your work."

"Thank you," said King.

"It's something to believe in," continued Martin. "It's so hard to believe in *anything* anymore, you know? Like religion. You can't really take it seriously because it seems so mythological and arbitrary. On the other hand, science is just pure empiricism and, by virtue of its method, excludes metaphysics. I guess I wouldn't believe in *anything* if it weren't for my *Lucky Astrology Mood Watch*."

King had heard the joke before, but he tried to smile. "Praise from you means a great deal. I'm a big fan of your films. Particularly the earlier, funny ones."

Martin smiled enigmatically and disappeared back into the large Victorian summer home.

"So Steve Martin works for you?"

"He's an associate. I need well-p-p-placed friends to carry out the work I do."

"And what exactly is the work you do?" King sipped the wine. It really was quite good. He shouldn't be drinking, but, what the hell? This was the end of the line.

Liguori chuckled and stroked his moustache, the sun burning across his bald head. "I *relocate* people."

"And the dead bodies who've been discovered? The ones who are altered to look like the writers? Where, may inquiring minds ask, do they come from? Does Igor abduct them from the cobbled streets of London?"

"As I said, I relocate people. Both the living and the d-d-dead."

"Are you a grave robber or a murderer?" asked King.

"You seem f-f-fascinated by *t-t-technicalities.*"

"I'm a writer. I like to get the details right."

"Have some more wine, Mr. King. Then we'll get to the d-d-details."

"One more question. What's in the briefcase?"

Liguori tapped the aluminum attaché case. "Your contract. You don't think we'd do anything without a contract, do you?"

"A contract to disappear?"

"You need a contract to donate 50% of your estate to the Swan's Island N-N-Nature Conservatory in the event of your untimely d-d-demise."

"Fifty percent?"

"Oh, we think that's m-m-more than fair. When you consider what your estate must generate? The enduring value of your c-c-copyrights? At 50% your family will be well t-t-taken care of. And the remaining 50%? Well?" He gestured to the beauty of the island all around them. "Who doesn't love nature?"

They were walking across the sloping, immaculately groomed lawn. In the center of the lawn was an old-fashioned iron pump with a cedar bucket. Liguori pumped some water and splashed his face. "Artesian well water." He took a drink. "C-c-coming to you straight from Maine."

Then there came a most curious sound from the hill behind them. It was *singing*—the sort of rhythm-and-blues close-harmony singing one associated with vocal groups from the 30s and 40s. It grew louder, and with it came the sound of roller skates or rollerblades. King looked up towards the rim of the hill to see, flashing through the overhanging branches, the figures of four black men wearing white suits with black bowties. Black handkerchiefs protruded from their breast pockets. They were not walking—they were skating on the paved path at about ten miles per hour. They were humming now, in beautiful harmony, and one of them was speaking in rhythm:

"If I didn't care, honeychile, more than words could say. If I didn't care, would I feel this way? Darling, if this isn't *love*, then why do I *thrill* so much? And what is it that makes my head go round and round, while my heart just stands *still* so much?"

King blinked his eyes in disbelief. "Holy Christ, don't tell me the Ink Spots are living here!"

"No," said Liguori, now also looking at the top of the hill. "The Ink Spots are long gone. These are the *Ink-bots*."

"Robots?"

"Sort of. They're a kind of c-c-cybernetic s-s-security force that patrols the Compound night and day. Armed with laser weapons. We obviously can't risk having any s-s-strangers wandering around this place."

"And they sing?"

King's voice must have been detected by the Ink-bots because in one instant the singers stopped, and the four well-dressed robots stood stock-still, turned, simultaneously drew four long, electronic-looking weapons, and aimed them precisely at King. He caught a glint of the sun against the barrels.

"It's okay, Bill," Liguori spoke urgently into what looked like the cell phone he had plucked from his belt. "Ivory, Charlie, Orville—he's okay."

With no hesitation the robots were rolling again, singing mid-sentence, as if the digital music players in their heads had simply been paused for a second.

Bill Kenny, the ethereal-voiced tenor, threw out his arms to sing the last line of the lyric:

And would I be sure that this is love beyond compaaaaaaare!
Would all this be true,
If I didn't care for you?

And the group skated into the hills.

"The singing is our little j-j-joke," said Liguori.

"Who's this 'our'?" asked King. "Who runs this place?"

"My brother does," said Liguori. "Unfortunately he cannot speak, so I handle the t-t-technicalities."

A graceful baby deer stepped into the clearing: lovely and tentative on frail legs. It looked like a brown greyhound.

"My brother concerns himself more with nature."

There was a swift, deadly-sounding whipcrack, like a sort of karate blow, and the deer was down on the ground. Instantly at its neck appeared—how to describe it?—a sort of man: large, nearly seven feet tall. White shirt, black trousers, it crouched over the poor animal. King couldn't see its head, and it was tearing the deer apart with its teeth. It was eating the deer alive.

The man must have caught the scent of King, because it turned to face him.

King literally stopped breathing. His hand went to his mouth.

The thing indeed possessed the body of a massive man, but its head was that of an enormous lizard: large black eyes, a protruding beak spiked with terrible teeth. A man with a dinosaur's head. An ancient iguana's head. It's nose-holes flared at the smell of King. Its mouth opened slightly and blood dripped onto its white shirt. It cocked its head quizzically at King.

King stood frozen to the spot.

"Mr. King," said Liguori. "May I p-p-present my unfortunate brother."

The last image King's eyes registered was the creature leaping towards him.

***

King awoke to a woman in her seventies placing a blue plastic icepack on his forehead.

Sunlight streamed into what felt like a convalescent room. The trees outside the window suggested he was still on the grounds of the Compound.

"Poor baby," said the woman, and it took King a full minute to realize he'd seen her before: soulful, compassionate, still beautiful.

"I think I fainted," said King.

"You didn't faint," said the woman in a broad New York accent. "It was the drink, my dear Hamlet, the drink." She looked at him with a street-wise twist of her lip. "Haven't you learned yet that when the bad guy says, 'Try the wine,' you're gonna end up with your face in the spaghetti."

"You're Anne Bancroft, aren't you?"

"I'm not her grandmother's pet poodle."

"I thought you were—"

"Not dead. *Stunned!* I faked it like the rest of them." She adjusted the fresh flowers in the room. "I'm fine. I just needed to get away from Mel."

King considered this for a moment.

"I would've thought living with Mel Brooks would've been continuously entertaining."

"*Relentlessly* entertaining," Bancroft corrected. "And I mean that in the most *exhausting* way possible. You know what Mel's got? He's got this sort of Jewish Tourette's. *He can't stop!* You put *anything* in front of him, he just *annihilates* it with a joke. It's his automatic response to the world, and it never stops; never for one minute. We go out to eat; the check comes, he says: 'Don't accept it. It's just their first offer.' He asks what I'm ordering. I say: 'The free-range chicken looks good.' He starts in right away: 'I don't like that term *free-range*. It gives the chicken too much hope. Better it should say: *suffocated, strangled chicken.*' Now, okay, the first time you hear that shtick? Very funny. Maybe even the tenth time: 'Don't accept it. It's just their first offer'—but, listen to me, for Christ's sake: ten *years* of that shtick; twenty years; *forty years*—I want to kill him; I want to scream: *Just shut the fuck up about the chicken!* So I faked my death." She shook her head. "He was probably doing shtick at the funeral." She did her Mel Brooks voice: 'You know, this funeral cost more than the wedding? I shoulda skipped the marriage altogether, gone *right* to the funeral. I coulda saved half a million dollars, and saved myself writing all those Goddamn thank you notes. *Thank you for your generous savings bond of twenty-five dollars, you cheap Nazi bastard.* I wonder if I have to write thank you notes for the *funeral* now. *Oy a klug.* To the gravedigger: *The way you handled that shovel was so professional. Thank you so much.*'" She held her head. "I loved him, I really did, but enough is fucking enough."

"And you don't mind living here? On an island? Away from everything you know?"

She thought about this as she adjusted the bedspread. "I miss the bread at Nate 'n' Al's. You can't get that kind of really *soft* rye bread in Maine. It's just too goyish here. Too *spectacularly Gentile* as Mel would say. But I like the quiet. I really do. I like the sound of the crickets. I like that if you listen at night you can hear the ocean. It's as if you're hearing a message. Oh, and speaking of messages, your wife asked me to give you this." She reached into her Maine Public Radio bag. "She said you'd been trying to finish this all year." Bancroft pulled out the paperback of *Madame Bovary* that he had been struggling through. It was not *a* copy of *Madame*

Bovary; it was *his* copy—right down to the yellowed pages and *S. King* written in red ballpoint on the first page. He was supposed to lead the Bangor Men's Book Club in the fall. He'd written inside the cover:

—miniaturist

—observant/metaphorical

—small sensory details that mirror the larger mood of the scenes

"Thank you."

An idea occurred to him, and he tried to use conversation to misdirect Bancroft's attention.

"Tell me about that thing I saw. Did he say it was his *brother*?"

"Oh, *him*," said Bancroft. "I'm afraid that *is* his brother —well, sort of. It's a little complicated to explain...."

She began her story, and King pretended to be idly riffling through the pages of *Madame Bovary*. He stopped casually at page 23. This was where the secret messages between Tabby and him had always begun; the romantic game they'd been playing since he was actually 23.

Dead center and slightly to the right of the page was the phrase *three-franc coin*. With a blue pen she'd made a single dot under the *t*. He forced himself to memorize the letter because he was unable to write anything down. The code would run every third page.

"You know what an O.B.E. is?" Bancroft asked.

"Isn't that what John Lennon refused? Order of the British Empire?"

"Out of Body Experience," she said. "I would have thought you, of all people, would have known that."

"I'm just endlessly disappointing, aren't I?"

He flipped to page 26—left-hand page. On the

yellowed paper the phrase *Charles could stay no longer* had been coded with a single blue dot under the *h*.

She pulled her chair closer to his bed. "Are you listening to a word I'm saying? Or are you busy preparing your next joke like Mel?"

"I'm listening."

"Our host Michael Liguori is the great, great, great— God knows how fucking great—grandson of Alphonsus Liguori."

"Am I supposed to know who that is?"

King flipped to page 29. The *i* of *mistress* had been coded.

"Listen and learn, Mr. Master of the Macabre. Alphonsus Liguori was an Italian priest. This is a fairly famous story. In 1774 he was preparing mass when he suddenly blacked out. When he awoke he told the congregation that he had visited the deathbed of Pope Clement the fourteenth. Now Pope Clement was dying in *Rome*—that was a *four-day's* journey away. So, okay, he's just one more nutty Italian. Like my family. But now word comes back that, yes, indeed, Pope Clement had died, and the people beside him had absolutely and with perfect clarity *seen Liguori at the bedside.* Had spoken to him. Had joined him in prayer."

"Meaning?"

King turned to page 32. In *Sir Bartholomew* the *S* had been marked.

The first word was T-H-I-S. King's heart was hammering. Tabitha was speaking to him.

"Meaning he had been in *two* places at the same time. With *witnesses* at both locations. Are you hearing this? He was made a saint. It was one of the first authenticated case studies of *bilocation.*"

"Out-of-body experience?"

"Right. Like those people with near-death experiences who see themselves dying? As if they're floating somewhere up on the ceiling watching themselves being pronounced dead?"

Page 35 had two letters dotted in *Parisian*. I-S.

She'd been in a hurry—scared she couldn't finish the message. She was getting sloppy.

"The experience is nearly universal," said Bancroft. "The Norwegians have stories of the *vardoger*—the duplicate. The Scottish have *taslach*. In Cumberland there are apparitions called *swarths*, sort of shadow people who follow us. There's the old English *fetch*. The German *Doppelganger*."

"Fascinating," said King who was barely listening to a word of this.

He flipped to page 38. The *a* in *wheatfield* had been marked.

T-H-I-S-I-S-A-

"You're a writer. Think of literature. Dr. Jekyll and Mr. Hyde. Dorian Gray."

"Poe," added King. "Kafka. Dostoevsky. Didn't he actually write a story called 'The Double'?"

"Look at all this stuff Liguori left for you to read."

She pointed to the bedside table. King glanced at a pile of vintage magazines. There was the *British Journal of Medical Psychology* from 1934. An ace of spades had been inserted at an article called "The Phantom Double: Its Psychological Significance" by S.M. Coleman. King opened the article and saw that certain lines concerning Guy de Maupassant had been highlighted in orange: *As he was sitting at his table in the study...Maupassant turned round, and was not a little astonished to see himself enter, sit down...and told to dictate exactly what he was writing.*

From 1955, there was the *Journal of Nervous and Mental Disease.* A joker playing card was stuck in Todd and Dewhurst's "The Double: Its Psychopathology and Psycho-physiology."

Someone had written in the margin: *1955. Rejects Chomsky's UG!*

King said: "And you're really going to live here forever? You're willing to bring all that grief to your family just to be away from Mel?"

"First of all, my family," said Bancroft, "hardly exists anymore. The remaining few are probably as tired of me as I am of them. That sounds callous. But, you know, I *am* pretty callous. That's what getting old teaches you. Speaking of teaching: Liguori has me trying to teach that brother of his sign language."

"You're trying to teach *that* thing sign language?"

Bancroft rolled her eyes. "I think our host has been watching too many old movies."

"Having any luck?"

She lowered her voice. "Between you and me, it's like trying to teach a fucking fencepost. Are you hungry? I'll order you lunch."

She handed him a printed menu card. "We've got chicken or salmon."

"Free-range chicken?" he asked.

She shook her head. "I don't like that term: *free-range.* Gives the chicken too much hope."

King casually turned to page 41 of *Madame Bovary.*

The *t* in *top of a plump calf.* Page 44. The *r* in *Bovary.* Page 47. The *a* in *chance.*

It felt as if someone had turned up the thermostat in his heart.

T-H-I-S-I-S-A-T-R-A-

Page 50 contained no further marked letters. She'd been stopped.

"Excuse me," said King, moving his legs off the bed. "Christ, that hurts." He slipped on his Bean boots. "Look. I'll eat in a minute, but I've suddenly got this ferocious need to go to the bathroom."

Bancroft pointed to the door. "Down the corridor."

"This icepack feels great," said King, holding the gel-pac to his forehead. "Thanks so much. Be right back."

As soon as he was certain he was out of her range of vision, the icepack hit the floor, and he was running as fast as a man whose legs had been nearly crushed by a pick-up truck could possibly run.

Down the corridor.

Down the wide wooden stairs—to the second-floor.

The main lobby was empty except for a man in a blue mesh short-sleeved shirt, bending over what looked like the concierge's desk. He was talking on a cell phone.

Next to him, leaning against the back of a chair was a European-looking man with an artsy scarf around his neck and a lime-colored cashmere sweater.

King thought he vaguely recognized both of them.

He slowed down to appear casual as he strode towards the main door which was braced open like the door of a summer cottage. An old-fashioned door with the center all glass—the doorknob also glass, beveled like a prism—sparkling in the sunlight like an invitation.

King was certain the man on the cell phone was Kenneth Lay, the former Enron executive. Lay was chuckling into the phone: "I think Granny's gonna freeze *again* this winter."

"Morning," said King.

Lay gave him a two-fingered salute.

King moved towards the sunlight. He turned for a second to see the European-looking man with the scarf resume his conversation with Lay. The man in the scarf had a gentle voice and heavy French accent. "People are sentimental about their childhood memories," he was saying, "but most of the time childhood is a *nightmare* that you want to escape as soon as possible." And suddenly King knew who it was; the name seemed to enter sideways, the way memories often did. The man was François Truffaut, the "late" French film director. He was gray-haired now but very much alive. Truffaut continued: "A nightmare of no affections, a nightmare of solitude."

King stepped outside.

His head was on fire as he looked around into the blasting sun, this verdant paradise with its crickets and acorns.

François Truffaut, he thought. Jesus Christ, who else was here? Was Elvis in the kitchen preparing peanut butter and banana sandwiches? *Uh, thank ya, ma'am.*

Keep moving, Stephen, he told himself. *Just keep moving.*

Other parts of the island were populated with tourists: Swan's Island, Minturn, Atlantic. There had to be authentic bed-and-breakfasts on the island, there had to be *people* on the island, lots of them; he could escape in a kayak if he had to.

King was climbing uphill now.

There had to be police on this island.

Should he try to find Tabby? Should he try a single-handed rescue? What had Tabby told him? Women's brains were attracted by *bravery* not by *niceness.*

It was species survival. If you made her fresh-squeezed orange juice you were an ineffectual pansy, but if you broke through her wall to snake out her sewer line until your hands were black and you smelled like a two-ton shit, *then* you were worth fucking.

Okay, he'd prove to her he was brave.

How was he going to find her?

How was he going to rescue her from Monster Boy?

King was running through the woods now.

He had to get to the authorities.

Get off the island, Stephen.

Then call the F.B.I.

Then *The New York Times.*

Then Amy Goodman and *Democracy Now!*

Tell the authorities what?

"My wife put little dots into a copy of *Madame Bovary* that said: *This is a tra—*"

"This is a tra?"

"I'm sure she was saying *trap.*"

"How can you be sure, Mr. King? How can you be sure she even made these marks?"

"I'm *sure,* okay? What was she saying: 'This is a trapezoid'? *My wife is in danger.* Flood that island with investigators. There's a monster on the loose!"

That would make a convincing argument.

"Just the facts, ma'am. Just the *bare* facts."

The hill leveled into a paved path. It was strewn with acorns. He picked one up for good luck.

Acorns had been another part of the code between him and Tabitha. Acorns meant the finishing of another manuscript he'd written during the summer—and Tabitha's blessing of good luck for the book in the fall.

He moved beyond the path into the woods. It was harder going here: nature reclaiming the Compound. But he *had* to get to the more populated side of the island. He *would* find a phone. Lay had a cell phone that seemed to be working. There had to be some kind of police.

Everything around him looked like poison ivy. Every speckled spider on every tree trunk was dripping with Ebola. Marburg. Filovirus.

His hands hit something metal.

The fence at the perimeter of the grounds. It was well over his head, and the top was extended with two more feet of barbed wire.

He thought: *If I were younger I'd try to scale it*—then he thought: *You're 59, Stephen, and you still have to try.*

With his bad leg and his bad neck and his Bean boots. And how does he get over the barbed wire?

Cover it with your shirt.

He unbuttoned his shirt, and hung it out of his back pocket.

Stephen, what the fuck are you doing?

His Bean boots were too broad to get a toehold in the fencing. He undid his boots, tied the laces together, and hung them around his neck.

Then he started climbing.

Primitive man.

Naked man.

He was Ed in *Deliverance*. Climbing straight up that mountain to escape King Cornhole.

He was sweating and shirtless; he could feel his poor heart.

I'm too old for this.

His hands hurt. His upper body strength was pathetic; the accident had reduced him to an old man—an old woman in the grocery store: "Young fella, could you get me that small mayonnaise from way up there? I don't know why they put 'em up so high."

His toes, through his white socks, found at least some small purchase on the cyclone fencing, and he began to hoist himself up, foot by foot.

His left shoulder was killing him.

James Bond at 59, he thought. *Cut! I gotta take another pee. Sorry.*

He was up high enough to throw his shirt towards the top of the barbed wire where it stuck like a tattered flag. It barely gave him any protection at all.

But he was nearing the top.

Then there was a noise—ball bearings? No. Roller skates.

Then singing:

I like java sweet and hot,

Whoops, Mr. Moto, I'm a coffee pot!

He turned his neck painfully to see the white suits of the Ink-bots rolling along the paved path below and in front of him—their laser weapons drawn.

They passed.

No, they didn't.

They stopped. Swiveled on their pivots. Then they fired something orange and blast-furnace-hot at this neck.

Trick#14 in *Learn How to Be a Handcuff King and Mystery Man* is "Escape from Chair Trick."

The performer exhibits an ordinary chair and a piece of cotton rope. He then seats himself in the chair asking a committee, previously selected from the audience, to bind him to the chair. After the performer is securely bound, a screen is placed in front of him and in a comparatively short time he appears in front of the screen free from bondage.

The childhood memory of this pamphlet from the Johnson Smith Company was surfacing in King's brain as Liguori pulled a long rope tightly around him.

King was, indeed, tied to a chair, the cotton rope spiraling around his feet, his torso, his chest.

The magic book had instructed the performer to keep his legs *slightly* apart and to *expand* his chest muscles as much as possible while being tied.

King tried to throw out his chest like some absurd movie Tarzan as Liguori pulled the rope so tightly King felt all his breath leave him. He was still wearing no shirt and no shoes, and the back of his neck felt badly burned.

He sat in the center of a large, dim, circular room. It looked, to King, like an exhibition hall in an old museum. Maybe he *was* in an old museum: all around him, set into the walls, were thick glass windows, and behind each window was a natural setting of some kind—like the dioramas in the Museum of Natural History with their tapirs and Eskimos and anthills.

The ceiling was an enormous dark dome, and King thought the place must once have been an observatory. There was a join in the ceiling; at some point in its history it must have opened to the stars. Music softly reverberated from the walls: strange, breathy meditation music.

As King's vision grew accustomed to the dim light, he saw that the monster, the half-man, half-lizard, was moving about in the darkness. King could see his white shirt flashing and those liquid black eyes. He remembered the tattoo on the arm of the girl who had called the tow truck. He remembered the plastic figure in the truck.

Anne Bancroft held the monster's right hand in her own. She was trying to get its fingers to correspond to sign language.

"F-L-O-O-R," she said, and she moved his five clumsy fingers—more like talons than fingers. She forced his hand to the floor in an attempt to make a physical connection with the word. Then she said, "B-O-O-K," and from a small metal table lifted what King immediately recognized as a hardback copy of his own *On Writing* with its photograph of a yellow storm cellar door on the cover. She again forced the creature's hand to make the symbols and then pushed the actual book into its hands. It grunted in displeasure and threw the book to the ground.

"My b-b-brother Gori is not f-f-fond of reading," said Liguori, emerging from the darkness. The dim light reflected on his completely bald head.

Liguori picked up *On Writing* and turned to the author photograph of King after his accident: looking hurt, pale, shrunken, and cowlicked.

"Look!" said Liguori to his brother. He pointed to King—then pointed to the picture on the book jacket.

The monster moved forward and took the book in his claws. He looked at the photograph, then rubbed his sharp nails across it. Then he extended his claw and touched King's forehead. King could smell the creature's hand; it smelled like a turtle.

The face of the thing was that of a crocodile or a primitive reptile. It was moist and covered in scales. There were nose holes at the end of its beak. Tiny devil ears. And in its little black eyes something strangely human and panicked.

Then the monster flipped through the printed text—page after page—which seemed to increasingly infuriate him.

He ripped pages from the book. He made a terrible sound as if he were trying to speak, as if he were trying to scream.

"P-p-poor thing," said Liguori.

The monster placed what remained of the book on the small metal table; he disappeared for a second into the shadows, and returned with a thin black hose. King smelled kerosene. In an instant the monster was spraying the book, and in the next moment he returned with an ugly-looking black metal torch that shot an enormous swath of flame at the table. King could feel the heat against his chest. The monster manipulated the flame-thrower as if it were a fire hose, and King watched the pages of his "memoir of the craft" curl into black ash.

If the creature could be said to be smiling, then it was.

King closed his eyes to the heat and the smell of the kerosene and the terrible image before him.

"That's enough, Gori," said Liguori sternly.

Bancroft picked up a cedar water bucket from beneath the table and carefully extinguished the last bit of flame. Then she led Gori away into the darkness.

The smoking black book remained.

"He's not f-f-fond of writers," said Liguori. "They r-r-represent what he can't do. Which is to c-c-comprehend words."

"He's illiterate?" asked King.

"No. He was born apparently with the capacity for language."

"Can he hear?"

"We think he can. When he was younger he d-d-definitely could. I'm not so sure anymore. But it's why I keep this music playing."

Reverberating from the walls drifted down dreamy Zen-like music: a sort of breathing, synthesized sound; the music one heard in stores that sold metaphysical books.

"He was different when he was younger," continued Liguori. "I was told that he began talking when he was six months old. He could say 'water.' Well, he could say 'wahwah.' 'Wahwah' but he meant water; he knew what it meant. Or so my father believed. I believe it's still inside him somewhere."

"Was he born looking like that?"

King was trying to flex and unflex his chest muscles— searching for some slack.

"My father was a descendant of Alfonso Liguori, the founder of the R-R-Redemptorist Order, and like all those years ago in Amalfi when Alfonso fell into that trance and translocated to Rome, my father, too, was c-c-capable of what he called 'traveling clairvoyance.' Astral p-p-projection. Out of body experience. I believe the scientists now like to use the term 'lucid d-d-dreaming.'"

"I've heard of that." King felt he had worked some slack in both his chest and legs. *Keep the bad guy talking.* "They talk about it in that movie, *Waking Life*? What does astral projection have to do with the condition of your brother?"

"During one of my father's episodes of bilocation, the *other* version of himself, the so-called spirit version, apparently had sex with a shop girl in Portland. The girl was a virgin. She swore that it was immaculate conception. She was later institutionalized, poor thing." Liguori pointed into the darkness where his brother had stood. *"This* was her child."

"Astonishing," said King, who didn't believe a word of it. Some poor teenaged shop girl in Portland gets knocked up in the Sixties, King imagined, tries to give herself a Drano douche, and this walking abortion is the result.

Or else she was fucking a crocodile.

"After six months or so my brother lost all c-c-capacity for language," said Liguori. "Chomsky told my father after the third year that it was impossible. That the child's brain was not imprinted with what Chomsky called Universal G-G-G-rammar."

"What's Universal Grammar?" asked King. His right shoulder definitely had some slack. He thought that with enough work he might free his right arm.

...and in a comparatively short time he appears in front of the screen free from his bondage.

"Do you believe in God, Mr. King?"

"On good days I do."

"My father Alfonso Liguori, Jr. believed in God. It was the core of who he was. He rejected Chomsky's notion of a Universal G-G-Grammar. That is: that human beings are somehow *born* with the circuitry of language, that there's some deep-structure hard-wired inside our brains. Chomsky believed that humans, and humans alone, could learn language for the same reasons they grew arms instead of wings: that they were born that way, genetically disposed that way. The patterns came from *inside* us. But what my father believed was that those organizing patterns, those systems Chomsky called d-d-deep-structures, were coming from the *outside*. That we simply *perceived* the p-p-pattern, the intelligence, the structure of the universe that was all around us. We unconsciously *absorbed* the structure of an intelligent universe all around us, and *that's* why we could speak. In short, Mr. King, we learned how to speak from God. From an intelligence that pervades everything around us."

King found himself actually listening.

"When God wanted beautiful language, he imprinted that gift on an English country boy, and summoned forth William Shakespeare. When God wanted beautiful melody he imprinted that gift on a Jewish doctor's son, and brought forth Richard Rodgers. *Do you understand?*"

Liguori's tone was urgent—and there was some kind of crazy gleam in his eye.

In the meantime, King's eye had caught movement behind one of the glass windows in the walls. A man in a red windbreaker and a ball cap was watching him—hands cupped to the glass. King recognized the man as Tom Clancy.

If his heart could speak, it would have murmured *oh, fuck.*

A woman stood behind another one of the windows— primping at a mirror, adjusting her earrings.

It was Danielle Steel.

"Chomsky told my father that this poor, strange, deformed son of his would *never* speak. Would never read, would never understand. He would be imprisoned forever. Chomsky said my brother lacked the wiring, the Universal G-G-Grammar of syntactic structures. Chomsky told my father to destroy the monster. That's what he called my brother: a monster. But my father b-b-b-b-believed in a God that could do *anything.* My father believed in a universe f-f-filled with miracles."

"Why have you kidnapped these writers?"

"I've kidnapped them because it is my brother's wish."

King felt another two inches of manipulation would free the fingers of his right hand.

"It's your brother's wish to torture these men and women."

"No one's being t-t-tortured here, Mr. King."

"Is my wife here? Did you kidnap my wife? She's done nothing to you."

"We took her to lure *you* here, Mr. King."

King's right wrist was loose and with those fingers he scrabbled at the knots holding his left wrist.

He tried to rub the rope against one of the nails on the chair back, but there was barely any abrasive surface. Still he rubbed it.

"To torture me?"

"No one's *torturing* anyone here, Mr. King." He gestured to the various windows (*cages,* thought King) that lined the room. "Everyone's happy. Everyone's healthy. Everyone's *normal.* They just can't *write.* They just can't *speak* to one another. They each have a beautiful cherry wood desk. And not a single pen. Isn't that tragic? And not a single piece of paper. And not a radio. And not a telephone."

"It's sick," said King.

Liguori slapped King's face hard.

"It's *justice.* My brother wants them to feel what he feels. He wants these *fountains* of language, these monsters who won't *stop* writing; he wants them to feel what it's like to be locked up inside yourself forever. To be eternally silent. To be eternally *unpublished.* Night and day. Like my brother is. That's why you're here." He gestured to all the writers. "You're here because of an unjust God who has denied my brother what he longed for most. The gift of communication."

"Yeah, well, *fuck you!*" yelled King. "That's my gift of communication!"

He had pulled himself up, and shook himself half free from the ropes. He ineffectually elbowed Liguori in the chest and spun around; his feet were still partially tied to the chair.

"Tabby!" he screamed as loud as he could.

He lumbered towards the door, and he found himself face to face with Gori the Mute whose lizard countenance was so close King could actually feel the warmth of his breath and smell that terrible turtle smell.

Gori's mouth was open. King could see the black ridges that lined the roof of his mouth.

Then the music—that unnerving Zen meditation music that had softly reverberated in the room—suddenly went silent.

The lanyard in his pocket printed with the black and white bobwhites began vibrating like one of those electronic signal-boxes restaurants give to customers waiting for a table.

Somewhere outside the room came the sound of an explosion. A flash of light from the roof.

Liguori looked towards the ceiling. He seemed to sense that something was going terribly wrong.

And something astonishing *was* happening. The join in the dome of the roof was separating; the old machinery of the observatory grinding back into reluctant life—the pure blasting afternoon sunlight forcing its beautiful way into the room in an ever-widening stripe. Bright blue. Gori was shrinking into the corner like a vampire hiding from the approach of morning.

Then the startled silence of the room was suddenly replaced by a different type of music: a 1930s swing band, and a female vocalist who might have been Mildred Bailey:

Mr. Bob, don't you know things have changed?
You're behind time with the melody you always sing.
All the birds have their songs rearranged,
Better get smart, whatcha gotta do today is swing!
Through the widening crack in the ceiling came two

figures sailing in on black suspension wires. King thought they looked like some kind of fantastic Tom-Cruise-in-*Mission-Impossible* action figures, but instead of flying in black leather jumpsuits, the two men were dressed in blue jeans, suspenders, and broad straw sunhats jammed down onto their heads. The music boomed out:

I was talkin' to the whippoorwill,
He says you got a corny trill,
Bob White!
Watcha gonna swing tonight?

Despite their rustic garb, the Bob Whites landed with perfect military-assassin precision—their black sniper rifles drawn and aimed at Liguori.

"Freeze!" yelled Bobby. "Homeland Security!"

Liguori reached for his holstered pistol, and he had it halfway drawn when he was shot twice in the brain by the two brothers. Their weapons were nearly silent.

Two small bleeding holes appeared in Liguori's forehead, and he fell, bewildered, to his knees, as Mildred Bailey continued singing:

Even the owl
Tells me you're fowl,
Singin' those lullabye notes.

Then from deep in the shadows came a terrible white sizzling, smoky flash—like a burning magnesium ribbon.

Some kind of laser weapon had been fired.

Bob Whyte fell down in a crumpled heap. Then came a second smoking flash, and Whyte's brother screamed and fell inert on the floor.

The barrel of the laser weapon was still glowing a pale, bluish white when the man holding it emerged from the darkness. He was wearing enormous size-20 clown shoes. His white shirt and white hair glowed as the hard sunlight poured through the open ceiling.

"Her-her-her-HER-her!" he laughed.

It was Steve Martin.

A terrible howling arose in the room—an animal noise. It was a desperate and dangerous cry.

"Gori!" cried out Bancroft.

The creature was howling wildly. It stood paralyzed in the room staring down at the body of his dead brother. The body was now pooling in blood on the floor.

"Gori!" shouted Bancroft again, but the creature couldn't hear.

It held its hands to its ears as if to shut out the horror of the world. It spun in half circles like someone trying to pray. Its huge black eyes were pouring with tears.

It bent down to the body of its brother and touched the bleeding forehead. Then it raised its head to the ceiling and lifted its arms and cried out in a heart-rending howl.

Bancroft, in a desperate attempt to break the creature out of its incoherent anguish, again shouted, "Gori!"

The creature had taken Liguori's pistol and held it now to its own head.

"Gori, don't!" yelled Bancroft, and grabbed the cedar bucket and threw water on the monster.

The creature stood there a second: desperate, dripping, astonished, furious, broken.

Bancroft, as she had done a thousand times before, on automatic pilot now, forced the creature's hand to spell in sign language. "Water. W-A-T-E-R," she said. "Water. It has a name."

And then the miracle happened. The monster stood transfixed. It touched the water on its face, and with it King could see a change in the creature's face, some light coming into it he hadn't seen before, some struggle in the depths within it; and the creature's lips trembled, as if trying to remember something the muscles around them once knew. And at last, emerging painfully, there arose a baby sound buried beneath a lifetime of muteness.

"Wah. Wah," said the creature. Then again, with great effort. "Wah. Wah."

The monster touched its wet shirt, its wet face. Then it spelled something with its own hand.

Bancroft moved forward and took the creature's hand, spelling a word.

"Y-E-S," she whispered.

She spelled it again.

"Y-E-S."

Bancroft fell to her knees to take the creature's hand, but Gori pulled it back, pulled it free, bewildered, sensing, perhaps, the enormity of its dawning consciousness. Then the creature dropped to the floor and touched it.

Bancroft took the creature's hand and spelled into it.

"G-R-O-U-N-D."

The creature spelled it back.

"Yes!" said Bancroft. "Oh, my dear Gori."

The creature turned towards the body of Liguori. Then it held out its hand. Bancroft made its fingers spell and she said, "B-R-O-T-H-E-R."

The creature spelled it back.

"Yes! Yes!"

The creature, half crying over its brother, half crying over its own discovery, turned to the metal table where there still lay the charred remains of *On Writing*.

"B-O-O-K," Bancroft signed.

The creature repeated the sign. Then it flipped the surviving pages of *On Writing*. It pointed to the small black lines of print. It held out its hand.

Bancroft signed: "W-O-R-D-S."

The creature flipped to another page.

Bancroft signed again: "W-O-R-D-S."

The creature signed back: "W-O-R-D-S."

"Yes!"

Finally, the creature turned to what remained of page 68 of *On Writing* and pointed to the words.

Bancroft looked at the text: *which dissolved when the hot water hit them...*

She moved the creature's finger directly to the individual word *water*, then she forced his hand to spell: W-A-T-E-R.

Gori looked at the text. Looked directly at the word. Rubbed his finger on the word. Then rubbed his finger on his wet shirt.

"Yes, Gori!"

Then he rubbed his finger again on the word.

"Yes!"

Gori threw back his head to the heavens and cried.

During the distraction of this strange tableau, King had managed to wriggle out of his remaining ropes. He approached Steve Martin from behind—joined his hands together like a hammer and clocked Martin in the skull with all the strength he had.

Martin went sailing sideways, clomping ridiculously in those clown shoes before he fell to the floor. He'd dropped his laser weapon which King instantly snatched up. It was still warm and it was much lighter than he'd imagined.

He aimed it directly at Martin's head.

"Why are you doing this?" asked King.

Martin was pulling at his collar, gasping for breath. Still lying on the floor, he said, "Why am I doing this, you want to know? Why me—*a smart facile thinker with a serious reach*? Okay, I'll tell you why. And I know this sounds like the obligatory villain-explains-himself-before-he's-killed-speech, but I'm going to say it anyway. Okay. I get a script in the mail a month ago from my agent. A Post-it note attached. *Steve— This may not be ROXANNE but think about doing it just to keep your name in the public.* You know what it was? *Cheaper by the Dozen III*! Jesus Christ! Okay, I thought I couldn't get lower than remaking *The Pink Panther.* I mean, let's go out and remake *The Gold Rush*! Let's remake *The Bank Dick*! Is every great comedian replaceable for the *Jackass* generation? The generation that thinks taking a dump in a Home Depot toilet is the pinnacle of artful self-expression? I just couldn't take it anymore. I looked at that script. I told myself: I'd rather be henchman to a psychotic lizard hell-bent on torturing every bestselling author in America than be in *Cheaper by the Dozen III.* Christ, I've got *some* pride."

"Save the speech for your Kennedy Awards show highlights reel," said King. He armed the laser rifle. "I don't know if this is going to kill you or stun you, and, frankly, I don't give a fuck."

King pulled the trigger. The rifle made a noise that sounded not so much like a *whoosh* but a *wazmo!*

A blue-white lighting bolt leaped out at Martin's head—and suddenly his body was ten feet away on the floor, his neck arched back, his mouth open, smoke pouring from his collar.

King felt like Rambo.

Women wanted to fuck guys who were brave, he remembered.

He aimed the rifle at the upper edge of Tom Clancy's windowed cage. *Wazmo!* The thick glass exploded.

"That's nice shooting, soldier!" yelled Clancy, and he leaped out to the floor—he moved immediately to the Bob Whytes and retrieved one of their sniper rifles. "There's two of us now, dude."

King's next shot shattered the window imprisoning Danielle Steel.

This broad would fuck me in a heartbeat, thought King.

She'd say: *Oh, Stephen, how can I ever repay you?*

And he'd look at her with all the love in his heart and say, *Stop writing.*

The next blast shattered the window imprisoning Curtis Sittenfeld, who stepped out through the smoke, surveyed the strange scene before her—the monster, the teacher, the shattered glass, the drawn rifle, the blue sky above—and thought: *Nobody reads the daily review anyway. And Random House has got enough blurbs so they could run a full-page ad just with the advanced praise.*

The next window held a young man in a top hat and an old black Dickensian clerk's suit with a white ruffled shirt. He wore a badge that read #48. King couldn't quite place him, but he knew he'd seen him before. He was handcuffed to a support post inside his bedroom, and was singing: *Dem bones, dem bones, dem dry bones!*

A blast from the laser rifle shattered the glass.

The young man tipped his top hat (as best he could) to King. "I'm born all over."

The next window lovingly destroyed was Sue Grafton's, but, unfortunately, she missed the entire show as she was sitting in her private bathroom sweltering in yet another attack of massive diarrhea.

There was one remaining occupied window on his left.

"I love my love!" King shouted, and he blasted the glass to pieces.

There was silence. Falling glass.

From the smoke and the rubble stepped Tabitha King.

She was dressed in her red sweater. She looked like a cardinal. The dark tendrils of her curly hair framed her wide, curious, even amused eyes. She looked exhausted; he could see the shadows under her eyes.

They stared at each other for a moment.

And the music in the room suddenly changed from "Bobwhite" to what sounded like an old German 78 r.p.m. record: *Mein Liebling, Mein Rose.*

She sighed. "...Stephen...It's been quite a night...."

And he, as John Steed, replied: "Well, it's morning now...the fog's lifted...let's get a breath of fresh air."

He lifted her in his arms. She kissed him.

Then he had to put her back down. She probably needed to lose a little weight.

"My proposal," said François Truffaut that evening at dinner—a dinner that Truffaut himself had lovingly prepared—"is that you reconsider your immediate, your automatic impulse to go home."

The writers were assembled around two wooden tables that had been moved together on the lawn of the complex. The sun was setting; the air was cooling down.

The two Bob Whytes were lying on chaise lounges near the long table. They were injured but remained in good spirits.

Steve Martin was dead.

Liguori was dead.

Kenneth Lay had escaped on a motorboat.

At the head of the table sat Gori next to Anne Bancroft. She translated his hand gestures. Bancroft was explaining that she didn't like the term "free-range chicken."

At the opposite end of the table stood Truffaut.

"Let us propose a toast," said Truffaut. "And a proposal *modeste*."

Sue Grafton, Tom Clancy, Danielle Steel, and Curtis Sittenfeld raised their glasses of white wine. Stephen King's arm was draped adoringly around Tabitha—and together they raised their glasses. He noticed, with some affection, that she still put ice cubes in her wine.

"To our generous host who used to be called Gori the Mute, and must now be called Gori the Articulate." Truffaut put the accent on the second syllable: Gor-EE. Bancroft translated the toast into sign language. "His malevolent and,

I think, deeply deranged brother now gone, Gori is granted the miracle of language, and becomes, I think, truly himself for the first time."

As Bancroft translated, Gori's eyes welled up, and he wiped them with his napkin. He raised a claw as if to say: *Please, no more.*

They all toasted Gori.

"But Mr. Gori cannot live among the multitudes of men," continued Truffaut. "Like Victor de l'Aveyron, the wild child in my film *L'Enfant Sauvage*, Mr. Gori was raised without the constraints and prejudices of society. To throw him into that world now would be impossibly cruel. He would be ostracized; he would be held in captivity; he would very probably be killed. Monsieur Gori chooses, if I understand him correctly, to remain on the island, to retain the Compound as his home. Frankly, I do not blame him."

"Hear, hear."

Truffaut adjusted the black ascot he'd tucked beneath the collar of his lime-colored cashmere cardigan.

"I couldn't stay here one more second," said Steel.

"Why not?" asked Truffaut.

"Listen, Sweet Pea, you're a marvelous man, and, believe me, if you were a little younger I'd be setting my cap for you, but as to your offer, I'm going to have to plead 'no contents.' I've got my art gallery. I've got my charity signing in Sausalito next week, and I need to change the dedications on some of my backlist."

"Very well, Madame Steel, you are free to do what you must."

"And in my trade," said Clancy, "the espionage novel, you've got to be cutting edge. I mean le Carré is still publishing. Year after fucking year. My stuff is going to sound stale."

"And I want to see my boyfriend," added Sittenfeld.

They all turned to her as if to say: *What boyfriend?*

"Brad? I gave him an *acknowledgement* in *The Man of My Dreams?* He's saving the *Sunday Times Book Reviews* for me. I wanted to check if my...if my choices...if...what the top 100 books were...selected from recent fiction. A.O. Scott *asked* me to vote for—I was probably the *youngest* person he asked."

"You're also free to do as you wish," said Truffaut. "But consider, for a moment, the unique situation that brings us here.... Our families think we are dead. In many cases they've already *grieved* for us. Held elaborate memorials. Are you really going to show up now on their doorsteps and say, 'Not only am I alive, but I agreed to fake my own death to escape *you*.' Now, true, that promise of escape turned out to be a desperate hoax—but it was an escape we all seriously considered. I certainly did. It was the ruse that got me, that got nearly all of us, to this remote place. And once I was here, and saw the horrible imprisonment of the writers, I chose—and I am more deeply ashamed of this than anything else I've done in my life—I chose to labor for my captors in order to stay alive and free. I was like the poor Jews in the camps who sold their souls to stay alive. I hope someday you may be able to forgive me."

"I, too, am guilty of betraying you," said Bancroft. She wiped tears from her eyes.

She translated for Gori who shook his head and furiously signed back to her.

"He says, 'You must forgive yourselves. It is I whom you must blame.'"

"No, no!" cried the table.

"It wasn't you!"

"It was your brother."

"Blame your brother."

Bancroft translated: "He says, 'I allowed it.'"

"No, no!"

"Monsieur Gori is right in that we must all forgive ourselves," said Truffaut. "All of us."

"Except for Ken Lay, that slimeball," said Clancy.

"Yes, yes," said Truffaut. "Except for Ken Lay. Him we must *never* forgive, as long as humanity beats within us. But my proposition is simply this: *Let us remain here.* All of us. Together. Hidden from the world. Hidden from responsibility. Hidden from income tax! And rapacious spouses! And ungrateful children! Look. Liguori already disposed of our estates. Half to our families, half to the Nature Institute of Swan's Island which is now, for all intents and purposes, *us.* We can live here, in this secluded paradise, on our royalties. Our families are generously provided for. And we can live here in near perfect freedom. Free to think, free to write, even free to publish. *Posthumously!* Think about it, please! Paradise beckons if we are wise enough to grasp it."

Snow was falling. This pleased Truffaut enormously because it filmed so beautifully. He walked through the woods in a long woolen coat that looked as if it once might have belonged to an American detective. He wore the Borsolino hat Goddard had given him. Next to him trudged Gori, easily carrying a heavy tripod mounted with a high-definition video camera. Shooting on HD video allowed Truffaut to bypass film labs completely.

All of the writers had stayed. At least for that first winter. At night they lit fires; they sledded in the hills. It felt like a cross between a ski resort and a writer's retreat.

As more books became electronic entities, and as the Internet fell increasingly under the control of right-wing regimes bent on eliminating free speech entirely, Truffaut felt it imperative that the members of the Compound memorize books. They would become a living library that would endure media conglomeration and corporate monopoly. Swan's Island would be the last outpost of the freedom of art, and Truffaut would document the process.

He and Gori walked through the gently falling snow with the camera and tripod trying to get as many set-ups as they could.

Walking by a frozen stream, they filmed Tom Clancy in his black coat and Russian hat. He walked alone, reading aloud from the novel in his hands:

"*The Russia House.* By John le Carré. 'In a broad Moscow street not two hundred yards from the Leningrad station, on the upper floor of an ornate and hideous hotel built by Stalin in the style known to Muscovites as Empire During the Plague....'" Clancy laughed outloud. *"This guy's pretty good!"*

"Coupez!" shouted Truffaut. This two-syllable bark, Clancy imagined, was French for "cut." It sounded like *koo-pay.*

From the other side of the frame Sue Grafton entered reading aloud from a paperback. *"Seven Weeks to a Settled Stomach.* By Dr. Ronald Hoffman."

The snow was falling hard now. Stephen King was sitting by himself in an empty gazebo. The snow was pouring in.

As Truffaut filmed him, King turned to the first page of the novel he held in his thick winter gloves. The snow was gathering on his beard; he could feel it melting against the warmth of his skin.

"Action!" said Truffaut.

"Small World," read Stephen King. "'A novel by Tabitha King.'" He turned the page. "'To my own Boogieman.'"

His eyes welled up with hot tears.

"Coupez!" called Truffaut.

In the last remaining thirty minutes of daylight— magic hour, Gori called it—Truffaut found Curtis Sittenfeld in a hooded parka standing in a grove of birch trees. The trees contrasted memorably against the whiter snow. *A watery Wyeth wash,* thought Sittenfeld, but then rejected the phrase as too self-consciously alliterative.

The pale pink ribbon on the cover of her novel contrasted memorably with the white of her parka.

"Action!"

She opened the novel and read: *"Prep. A Novel. Curtis Sittenfeld.* Wait a minute."

"Coupez!"

She frowned. "Shouldn't I say *by* Curtis Sittenfeld? I mean, it doesn't *say* that, but don't you think it'd be clearer that I'm the author And that Curtis Sittenfeld isn't the name of the publisher?"

"Action!"

She frowned again.

"You know, I've got a work in progress that I think might be more appropriate for the film." She pulled out some handwritten pages from her coat. "I think *guys* might like this one a little better. What do you think?" She smiled. "My working title is *Looking For Mr. Twisty.*"

"Coupez!"

In a clearing near the shoreline Danielle Steel stood posing for an author photograph. Tabitha King was taking the photos on her small digital camera.

"Action!" called Truffaut.

Steel let her mink coat slip off her shoulders and, raising her arms, stood against the ice-edged evergreens in just her bra and panties.

"I'm not sure," she said. "Do you think this looks, you know, *posthumous* enough?"

"Coupez!"

At the sound of Truffaut's voice a flock of long-legged birds rose from the water. There must have been one hundred of them, silhouetted against the nearly lightless sky. Without a word gestured to him, Gori turned his video camera towards that mural of migrating birds:

preserving forever the visual record of their departure and the wintry cry of their voices.

"Did you get that?" asked Truffaut.

Gori turned from the viewfinder and used his clawed fingers to sign: "C-R-A-N-E S-H-O-T."

"Crane shot," translated Truffaut aloud.

And if reptiles could be said to smile, then Gori was smiling.

Truffaut felt his soul swoon slowly as he looked upon his friend, and he heard the snow falling faintly through the universe upon all the living and the dead and the Published.